WYSZKOWO, A *SHTETL* ON THE BUG RIVER

WYSZKOWO, A *SHTETL* ON THE BUG RIVER

By Adele Mondry

Translated from the Yiddish by Moshe Spiegel

KTAV PUBLISHING HOUSE, INC.
NEW YORK

© Copyright 1980
Adele Mondry

Library of Congress Cataloging in Publication Data

Mondry, Adele.
  Wyszkowo, a shtetl on the Bug River.

  Translation of A shtetl baym Bug.
  1. Jews in Wyszków, Poland (City)—Fiction.
1. Adler, Morris—Fiction. I. Title.
PZ4.M739Wy [PJ5129.M714] 839′.09′33 79-26259
ISBN 0-87068-657-7

Manufactured in the United States of America

To my husband Harry (Zvi)
of blessed memory
who encouraged and inspired me
to publish my work in Yiddish.
It is my regret
that he did not live
to see it in print.

CONTENTS

INTRODUCTION: IN REMEMBRANCE OF A WORLD THAT WAS

1.

Jewish life in Eastern Europe was not confined solely to the *shtetl*. There were sizeable communities in the large cities, such as Warsaw and Vilna, Kiev and Kishinev, and others. Indeed, they were called "Cities and Mothers in Israel," and special honor was conferred on Vilna; it was declared to be *Yerushelayim d'Litte*, the Jerusalem of Lithuania.

Yet Jewish life was concentrated mainly in the *shtetl* where the intrusions from the world *out there*—the pagan infiltration—were at a minimum and could be muted. In the *shtetl* the community could be more fully Jewish, and accommodation to the standards of the external world could be evaded. Tradition and custom regulated conduct, and piety was not primarily a mode of *believing* but a way of *living*.

The *shtetl* is no more. A monstrous enemy has destroyed it. Central and Eastern Europe—for Jews—is now a landscape of death, a vast cemetery. But even the image of a cemetery is inadequate, is merely a shadow of an actuality that is in its cumulative and comprehensive tragedy almost beyond expression. In a cemetery there are rows of graves in an open field, with grass around them and the blue sky above them. There are tombstones to mark the graves, and one could say *kaddish* or lay a wreath of flowers and touch the soil before departing.

In Auschwitz, Treblinka, Maidanek, and the other infernos there are no orderly rows of graves; the gas-ovens left us only ashes in the hand, a haunting memory in the mind, and anguish in the heart. In Auschwitz there are no tombstones, no grass, no blue sky and no stars at night, and one can recite only an inclusive *kaddish* for all the nameless men, women and children consumed in the crematoriums.

There must have been something in the *shtetl*—in the values and ideals that permeated it, in the atmosphere that enveloped it—that was precious, that was capable of sustaining the spirit and healing the heart, despite poverty and drabness and the imperfections which are inevitable in every society. It is not easy to define this "something," to apprehend its essence, to locate its highest level. Whatever else the *shtetl* may have been, it possessed a quality of wholeness and the people in it had a sense of rootedness, an abiding tradition, and a faith that absorbed and transcended despair. Above all, there was a common sharing of their mode of life; the fabric of the community was not riven and experience was not desultory, and the individual fitted into the rhythm and pattern of the community without losing his identity, without diminution of his selfhood.

2.

Wyszkowo, a Shtetl on the Bug River is the title of Adele Mondry's book of short stories. The word *shtetl* in the title remains untranslated, is kept in the original Yiddish. To substitute another word for *shtetl*—town, hamlet, village —would be almost like a falsification, like putting an alien mask on it. It would be a town, but not the town on the Bug River, the *shtetl* in which Adele Mondry spent her youth, where she caught the first glimpses of the reality and wonder and mystery of nature, where she learned—in Plato's phrase—to read the world.

That was a long time ago, and Adele Mondry's years in America, in Detroit, exceed by far her years as a girl in the town on the Bug River. But she is what she is because of the years in the *shtetl*, because she tasted of its sorrows and joys, because she cherishes the memory of its weekdays and Sabbaths, and because she loved its people. Love is of the heart, but for the wise and good it is also an organ of vision, and it transmutes *sight* into *insight*. Adele Mondry depicts the people of the *shtetl* with insight. She touches them as if with an enchanted wand, and restores the town on the River Bug, with the "dense forest that encloses it," as it was prior to the Holocaust. This is a literary achievement but it is also an act of reverence.

Adele Mondry left her *shtetl* sixty years ago—a little town in Poland. One might infer that her stories are parochial and provincial and hence of limited interest. In truth, it is not so. The measure of the universality of a piece of literature is the concreteness, intensity, and vividness of the people portrayed in it, of how much of life there is in it, and whether it contains—in Horace's beautiful phrase—*lacrimae rerum*, the tears of things. In Adele Mondry's stories there are the tears and smiles of things Jewish, the gentleness and sadness and hopes of men and women, as she perceived them with an "understanding heart." Her stories are of herself, of her grandmother, of her neighbors, who were very much like people in other towns, and surely different too, with a brightness of their own, with their own smiles and tears. The direction of the stories is outward, their "message" is not cryptic and obscure. They are her individual utterance, but not a private one.

It might be held that knowledge of the *shtetl* could be gotten more coherently and cogently from a study of history rather than from fiction. Wherein does history differ from literature? History is preoccupied with social causality, with the broad sweep of events, with aggregates of people, with humanity in its diversity—nations, classes. Literature is concerned with the causality of the heart, with ideas as embodied in experience, with individuals and particular things, with the tears of things, with *lacrimae rerum*. *Wyszkowo, a Shtetl on the Bug River* is a "slice" of history, but it is also a piece of literature.

3.

Adele Mondry's stories are of ordinary life in the *shtetl*, and yet there is a mythic quality in them. She begins with "ordinary life," with men and women in simple situations, devoid of unusual surprises, and elicits from them their divine spark, their *nitzutz* (in the language of Hassidism). The spark lights up the entire story and we behold in the ordinary that which is enduring, crystallized out of the very heart of Jewish experience as shaped by Jewish tradition.

Reb Sholem Refoelkes is a "plain" Jew, quite uncomplicated. The river of his life flows evenly, without turbulence. He is no traveler in the land. He observes the religious prescriptions as a matter of course; they are for him an integral component of the cadence and ritual of each day. But nothing was dearer to him than the Sabbath. To observe it was his supreme ecstasy. The legend of an "additional soul"—*neshamah yetera*—vouchsafed a Jew on the Sabbath, was for him reality. So it was before his marriage, and so it was during the fifty years afterward . . . and then he awakes one morning, dresses quickly, says his prayers, and hurries to his store. To his amazement, the marketplace is empty, there is stillness everywhere, and all the stores are closed, and Jews in their holiday clothes are going to the synagogue.

Reb Sholem had lost track of time, forgot that it was the holy Sabbath. His violation of the Sabbath shook him to the very roots of his being. For Reb Sholem, the bearer of a millennial tradition, his "error" was a disruption of the cosmic order. For one remote from the tradition as manifest in the milieu of the *shtetl*, the depth of Reb Sholem's dismay, his anguish of spirit, would be elusive, an effect widely out of proportion to the cause.

It is the merit of Adele Mondry's book that it is not a collection of sundry items, out of context, but a series of stories in which a Jewish town, its people, its atmosphere, are woven together in natural continuity. Reb Sholem is depicted as an individual, with his own signature, and yet as the bearer of tradition, incarnating one of the mythic elements in the tradition.

Not all the stories are idyllic, and in some the tradition is tarnished. In "Reb Bereleh" there is satire mingled with pathos. What might have been tragedy or melodrama is turned into a kind of comedy. Reb Bereleh is wealthy, generous, affable, and fond of moralizing about sexual purity. And then one night he seduces Tzireleh, his wife's maidservant. There was no premeditation, no shrewd scheming, no paroxysm of lust. There was a longing in Bereleh for a loveliness and a beauty that his wife never had. He approached Tzireleh in a mood of tenderness and caressed her with delicacy.

To say this is not to condone Reb Bereleh's offense, nor to dismiss his hypocrisy, nor to excuse his irresponsibility toward Tzireleh. This is the substance of classical tragedy. But Adele Mondry chose to do something else: to give us the pathos and comedy of a middle-aged man, in a community of piety and tradition, irresistibly pulled toward loveliness and beauty and the gratification of sensuous—not sensual—desire.

"Reb Sholem Refoelkes" was the vehicle for a mythic

element—the Sabbath—in the tradition, and "Grandmother Mirka" is a mythic figure, the matriarch who
rules the family. She rules indirectly, unobtrusively, not
so much by precept as by example, and her way is the
way of gentleness. Her vocation is to help the poor and
forlorn, for she knows that *tzedakah*, which is charity,
is derived from *tzedek*, which is justice. For grandmother
Mirka obligation blends into loving-kindness, and what
for others would be a duty was for her a song, a delight.

Grandmother Mirka is no abstraction. We see her
lighting the candles, with pensive eyes and shining face;
and we see her walking from street to street, from house
to house, with her alms-box for the poor. And it seems to
us—at least for a while—that grandmother Mirka is our
grandmother, too, the mythic figure, the wife and mother
in *Koheleth*, symbol of the courage and wisdom of generations of Jewish mothers and grandmothers.

4.

Wyszkowo, a Shtetl on the Bug River, consists of two
parts: the second is much shorter than the first, and
its locale is America, "on new soil," specifically Detroit.
The stories about the *shtetl* fall into a pattern, unified
in theme and content as by an invisible thread. Life
in the *shtetl* was invested with an order and a symmetry,
and the stories reflect it. In the perspective of time and
as sifted through the imagination, this order and symmetry attain a remarkable clarity.

There is no analogous *shtetl* in America. Jewish life in
America is variegated, pluralistic, and has not yet
achieved a distinctive style, a *nusakh* of its own. The
relation between the individual and the tradition, which
informed and nurtured our forbears, in Eastern Europe,
is here both ambiguous and ambivalent. Because Jewish

life in America is pluralistic and multi-faceted, there is a freedom of mind and an intellectual resilience, which generate and foster an independence of thought, but it is also a source of confusion, a cause of spiritual tension, and the individual is perplexed in the midst of a welter of pressures which impinge on him from all sides. America is "new soil" and the roots are still sinking in the soil, constantly but gradually.

"Before the Holy Ark" is a keen probing into the mind and soul of a young man, not yet twenty, unable to make the ascent toward the sun out of the labyrinth of Jewish actuality in America. The tone is elegiac but not oppressive, and there is in it the "sad, sweet music" of compassion.

The story is based on fact, on a terrible fact. One Saturday morning, in the presence of a full congregation, Richard, a young man of twenty, suddenly arose from his seat, went to the pulpit, turned toward Rabbi Morris Adler, accused him of cheapening normative Judaism, of converting its pure gold into the baser metals, of dispensing to his flock "packaged" religion. The stream of imprecation was like fire on his tongue, but before the fire cooled Richard waved a revolver, pulled the trigger and shot Rabbi Adler and then himself.

This is fact, but a fact does not explain itself, an event does not proclaim its import. It is the function of literature to illumine experience, to disclose and delineate the mystery and meaning of the fact. Without pretense and without vain speculation, but with psychological insight and artistic intuition Adele Mondry tries to get to the heart of this horrifying tragedy. Richard, she surmises, had been distressed by the assassination of President Kennedy and after much brooding, was inclined to interpret it as the act of one who adored Kennedy for what he should have been and abhorred him for falling short of it. Similarly, Richard loved and hated Rabbi Morris Adler—loved him for the vision of Judaism he had inspired in him, and hated him as a false prophet (in his fervid imagination), no longer equal to the ideal figure he had constructed out of his own longing and passion for perfection and blessedness.

It should be stressed, however, that Richard's deed was in contradiction to his own high concept of Judaism, to the commandment "Thou shalt not murder," *lo tirzakh*. Richard had himself succumbed to the pagan infiltration: to the idolatry of violence, to acquiescence in the principle of the fist. In the *shtetl* this could not have been: the cult of violence, the hegemony of force, the sovereignty of the fist, were alien to the system of values, to the categories of morality that guided and modulated both action and thought.

5.

I have dealt with these four stories so as to suggest the quality and scope of Adele Mondry's book, to indicate the character of the enterprise she undertook and carried through. It is fitting that I conclude my comments with a passage from her own introduction to the book: "I left the town where I was born in a turbulent and stormy time, during the Soviet Russian War against Poland. I was still relatively young then, and sentimental. I took along with me one small suitcase, a whole kaleidoscope of recollections—of the broad Bug River, the dense forest that encloses the town—and a nostalgic fondness for every nook and corner . . ."

Adele Mondry may have been sentimental, as a young girl should be, but in these stories there is solid, incisive sentiment. And the recollections are as fresh as this morning's dew, as pertinent as today's tears and smiles.

Her nostalgic fondness for what was and is no more, is not a truancy from the present but an enrichment of it, a bringing together of time and eternity. She wrote the stories in Yiddish, and her Yiddish is idiomatic, redolent of the aroma of the *shtetl*. And now we have it in English, in Moshe Spiegel's excellent translation, which preserves the flavor—the *taam*—of the original.

Israel Knox

A WORD FROM THE AUTHOR

I left the town where I was born in a turbulent and stormy time, during the Soviet Russian war against Poland. I was still relatively young then, and sentimental. I took along with me one small suitcase, a whole kaleidoscope of recollections—of the broad Bug River, the dense forest that encloses the town—and a nostalgic fondness for every nook and corner.

I cherished that store of memories more than the ten dollars a week that I was soon to begin earning in America. Perhaps this explains why I embarked on a different course from other immigrants at the time: Instead of studying English, I set about to perfect my knowledge of Yiddish.

My memories became even more precious to me after the town where I was born had been destroyed by the Nazi barbarians. The Jewish community was torn up, root and branch; there is not a vestige of it left. It has not been my intention, however, to write a book of memoirs. I merely wished to bring alive the Jewish home life, the Jewish characters, the Jewish cadence, from a way of life of which I had been and still am very much a part.

My literary debut came in 1921, when a Polish-language periodical in Detroit carried my account of the Soviet Russian war against Poland, at the time when the town changed hands.

Nothing remains of the small suitcase I brought with me to America. But the accompanying bag and baggage—the landscape and character of the town— have been preserved, and from time to time I have gleaned something or other from that storehouse. Under all sorts of conditions, even after I became the mother of two small children, I went on writing short stories about my birthplace. I would submit them to Yiddish newspapers in New York and to my pleasant surprise they were accepted and published.

Before long, a new idea took hold of me: I was reluctant to forfeit my credits for the six courses in high school I had taken at Wyszkowo, my birthplace, and so I took up my studies again, eventually graduating from Wayne State University. The result was that I stopped writing Yiddish for a decade. When finally I went back to my dormant manuscripts, two things became clear to me. One was that the subject of an entire Jewish town could not be exhausted in a single volume, nor by a single author, no matter how resourceful, and that therefore nothing was to be gained by waiting any longer to publish the account of my birthplace embodied in my manuscripts. Second, I saw that the evolution of Yiddish literature had brought with it stylistic change so considerable that I would have to revise my work before it could be published.

This volume is in two parts: the first, "Wyszkowo, a *Shtetl* on the Bug River," consists of short stories dealing with life before the Second World War in a Jewish town (*shtetl*) of Poland. Here I have tried to depict the townsmen and their ways, their ups and downs, the good times along with the bad. The narratives are largely concerned with actual events. The people who figure in my stories were familiar ones in the community, and can be recognized by the traits I have depicted. However, I have not adhered to literal fact in telling them. I have not set out merely to present a bare record, embellished by the author's imagination.

The second part, "On New Soil," is made up of narratives

concerned with the American-Jewish milieu. The series of events on which the central narrative, "Before the Holy Ark," is based are well known in the United States. A student's killing of the rabbi as he stood with his face toward the Holy Ark, delivering a sermon, came as a shock to American Jewry. I saw this horrifying event as a circumstance to be made into a story that would take its place in the realm of Yiddish literature. And I was to have no peace of mind until I carried out the task.

"Before the Holy Ark" is a psychological narrative with a profound insight. One or another phase that had been tacked on or deleted, in this instance is of minor importance. My intention was to portray the tragedy on a broad canvas, and to evoke the whole spectrum—that was the quintessence.

Aside from the impossibility of detachment, since the murdered rabbi was our friend, I was not sure whether the story ought to be told with the exact detail of a police report or with the intention of producing a work of art. I concluded that a faithful narrative would be the best tribute to the spiritual leader and sage who perished so tragically.

Adele Mondry

WYSZKOWO, A *SHTETL* ON THE BUG RIVER

REB SHOLEM REFOELKESS

At the beginning of their marriage, Kaila thought of herself as better at business than Sholem, her husband. Sholem lived by the generosity of his father-in-law, who provided room and board, as was the custom, so that Sholem could devote himself to the study of the Talmud without any worry over finances. Little consideration was given to his ability to carry on in business. Reb Alter Rashkess had entertained no illusions about his son-in-law's ability to earn a livelihood for his daughter, but had accepted him because he was sure that his daughter would take Sholem in hand and make a man of him.

Though the young scholar was welcomed and had perpetual maintenance, however, that arrangement came to an end after one year.

The income at Reb Alter Rashkess's grocery gradually declined, as new shops opened up and gave it competition; staying open at all hours in the hope of catching late customers. When it finally dawned on Kaila, the eldest daughter, that her father resented his son-in-law's endless hibernation in the House of Study, preoccupied with the Scriptures and coming home at nightfall just to eat, she went to her father and said, "Don't worry—God will not forsake me, any more than He forsakes the rest of his Jewish children. Somehow, in my own way, I will manage to make a livelihood."

The problem now was to find a suitable business for the son-in-law. Setting up another grocery was out of the question; there were already too many of those in the town. To open a drygoods store, one had to have the

3

wealth of a Korah—beyond Reb Alter Rashkess's means.
For a while he considered getting a license to sell wine
and spirits, or even beer. That would have been a
profitable business. However, for a Jew the difficulties
would have been almost insurmountable. It would have
been necessary beforehand to grease the palm of someone in the provincial capital, and also throw a sop to the
local commissar. So the only alternative was a grain and
produce shop, selling oats and grain to the draymen.

Kaila was well equipped for such a project: she could
lift a heavy sack, and was adept in handling the scale.
Reb Alter Rashkess welcomed the idea, and decided to
act at once: the younger daughters were growing up fast;
and with one son-in-law having to be supported, it was
difficult to attract bridegrooms for the other daughters.
He didn't have to look far for an opening. A vacant store
was available nearby, and he rented it for Kaila.

At first Sholem hardly set foot in the store. He would
come in for a minute or so, as a matter of duty. He would
see her hard at work, dragging the sacks of bran, buying
oats by the bag from peasants and emptying the grain
into the coachmen's narrow sacks, bargaining with the
peasants, and stooping to tie up the sacks. Sholem felt
obliged to lend a hand, but still he considered it beneath
his dignity to become a grain merchant. Sholem Refoelkess was a patrician born and bred; and if his parents had
known that Reb Alter Rashkess would provide no more
than this as a livelihood for the couple, there would have
been no marriage.

All the same, Kaila was pleased with Sholem as well as
with the store. For one thing, he was intelligent enough to
realize that without some sort of income life would be a
burden, and that his father-in-law could no longer be
depended upon to support him because of the two
daughters who were still unmarried. And since Kaila

didn't mind keeping the store on winter days, warming her hands over a charcoal brazier, he humored her for the sake of domestic harmony.

Gradually, Kaila drew him into a more active interest. From the first Sholem was uneasy at the thought of his wife being all day long in the company of peasants and wagon drivers. Seated before a volume of the Talmud, Sholem pictured her being harassed by crude peasants, and the draymen reaching out coarse hands to touch her; he imagined one of them accidently shoving her against a sack of oats, while the others reacted with bawdy laughter, so loud he could hear it in the House of Study. Increasingly disturbed by these thoughts he found himself impatient to finish his morning prayers so that he could rush down to the store. But he would find nothing untoward going on there. Kaila would appear perfectly at ease, work calmly, transacting her usual business with the peasants and teamsters. Sholem would berate himself for the vivid imaginings that had flashed before him above the fading pages, and would go back to the House of Study.

But the more Sholem frequented the place, the more he became intrigued by the business. He gradually became accustomed to the peasants who came to sell their grain. At times they seemed to carry with them the fragrance of warm milk and freshly mown hay. At close range the Jewish draymen appeared different from the way they had seemed at a distance, when he was on his way to the House of Study. He became aware that the stout, broad-shouldered Jews with their shaggy beards, their homespun jackets girdled in hemp, were bursting with good nature and simple kindness, ready to help Kaila in any way they could. So Sholem would set to work, dragging a measure of bran to the scales, and doing other chores, to show Kaila that he was willing to lend a hand.

Kaila beamed with delight at seeing her husband take the initiative. She knew that the time was approaching when she would need to be careful about lifting heavy sacks . . . She wondered whether Sholem would agree to take charge of the store, yet put off asking him. When she finally raised the question, however, he quickly said yes; and after a moment's thought, he made her promise that following her confinement, when she was able to work again, she would beware of desecrating the Sabbath. At the same time, he confided to her that business dealings all made him uneasy.

"Kaila," he said, "don't forget that Shmuel Laib is a more prominent merchant than I am. He is a prosperous lumber tradesman, he exports rafts to Danzig, and from there he imports goods worth thousands of roubles—yet he is a devout observer of the Holy Sabbath."

Very soon after their child was born, Sholem welcomed Kaila to the store with open arms. The place bulged with sacks of bran and oats, piled all the way to the ceiling. During Kaila's absence Sholem had installed a huge open grain pit to make things easier: it was now possible to ladle and scoop out the grain, instead of having to grapple with the sacks. That day, though it was only noon, Sholem had already transacted a good deal of business. He was eager to tell his wife all about having to be on the lookout for peasants who tried to make off with some grain, about having to hurry with his prayers, and about never having a chance on weekdays to pray with a minyan.* But he did not want to distress her unduly. So he told her instead about the new miller at the water mill, who had promised to supply flour products at a lower price, and of having the drovers address him respectfully as Reb Sholem and patronize none of the

---

*A prayer quorum consisting of ten male adults.

other merchants. Then he came to a matter of paramount importance—the same he had discussed with Kaila before her confinement but which she had presumably forgotten. So he lost no time in mentioning it.

"Kaila, there's one thing I have to bring to your attention," he said. "I don't suspect, God forbid, that you will desecrate the Sabbath by keeping the store open even one minute late. But I must impress upon you that the responsibility of observing the Sabbath is entirely incumbent upon the man—that is, upon myself. You are well aware that one engrossed in business can be tardy. So if you'll promise me to close the store in time to observe the Sabbath, even if it means you give up a little profit, I will devote myself wholeheartedly to the business every day until noon."

At first the whole thing sounded strange to Kaila: how could Sholem urge on her something that she herself approved of with all her heart? Hadn't she been brought up in a Hasidic household? And who could have been more punctilious in observing the Sabbath than her father? She suddenly returned to a fantasy from her childhood. She saw herself with her well-groomed braids facing the mirror on a Sabbath eve. Then she hopped into her bed, and no sooner had she fallen asleep than the country gentleman's son appeared with a riding crop in hand. But instead of raising the whip, he threw it away and kneeled before her, kissing her feet and gazing at her with such beautiful, imploring eyes . . .

Only now Kaila saw that Sholem likewise gazed at her with beautiful eyes, eyes as fine as the country gentleman's—perhaps even finer . . . She stretched out her hand to him, compelled to say, "Stand up, Sholem—I will behave as I did in my father's house as a child, when with my braids just washed, I lay in bed next to the wooden partition. Oh, Sholem!" she cried reproachfully.

"I will observe the Sabbath just as I did in my father's house!"

Once Sholem Refoelkess had finally become engrossed in the business, he lost track of the passage of time. It came and had gone again like a streak of lightning. Almost half a century had passed since he gave up his free room and board. Over a lifetime he and Kaila had brought up children and then grandchildren—who came each week to their grandparents for "Sabbath-oips," a treat of fruit and candy.

The little grain store is still in business, and now, half a century after he started to earn his livelihood, Sholem Refoelkess reminisces about all that he has experienced. He cannot enumerate the events that come crowding to his mind. But one thing delights him, he finds great security in it; he has kept his integrity. That thing has to do with not desecrating the Sabbath for the sake of business. Now it can be said, in summing up: "He was in business for half a century and he never once violated the Sabbath for mere profit."

It would be hard to depict how he trembled when Kaila first opened the grain shop and, later on, the apprehension felt as she drew him by degrees into the business. Many were the times when Satan took hold of the doorknob, as though gripping it with both hands, in his eagerness to tempt Sholem into desecrating the Sabbath. For it was just on the eve of the Sabbath, when the candles have to be lit, that peasants would come asking for bran and flour, which would have meant a great deal of profit. But Sholem would make a signal to Kaila, who could usually find a way of getting rid of the customers—by pretending that the scales were not functioning properly, or that she had an urgent matter to attend to. Asking her patrons to wait outside she would then lock the door, and rush home to light the candles and offer the benediction.

These were not isolated occurrences. Sholem had learned the strategem from Kaila, and he made use of it on a number of occasions. But one event is indelibly impressed on his mind—he has told it over and over to his children and grandchildren. Many years ago, on the "Short Friday,"* there had been a sudden thaw, followed by a drenching rain. Sholem kept looking impatiently at his double-cased, bulbous turnip-shaped silver watch, so as not to be late for the Sabbath service. As the downpour continued, the peasants covered their horses with blankets and sheepskin coats and came barging into the nearest stores. Sholem's now swarmed with them, the Sabbath was close at hand, Kaila was away, and he was at a loss about how to deal with the situation— which, even if he transacted no business was still tantamount to desecrating the Sabbath. Yet how could he turn the peasants out of doors in such vile weather? Suddenly, as though divinely inspired, he hit upon a novel idea: he would sacrifice a new tarpaulin that he had used to protect a wagonload of flour from the rain. Without further ado, Sholem offered his visitors the tarpaulin, so that they had only to step outside and stand under it as though it were a canopy.

The peasants, about a score of them altogether, were pleased with the notion, and lined up with the whips, going on and on over the offering, as though it had been manna from heaven, and they themselves were his equals. Sholem did not regret the sacrifice in the least, because Satan had been foiled in his purpose. And no sooner had the last peasant stepped out than Sholem locked the store.

He arrived at home dripping wet. Kaila urged him to change clothes. But he merely picked up his satin capote,

*The Friday preceding the winter solstice.

the long coat worn by orthodox Jews, and headed for the synagogue to usher in the Sabbath.

Following *Kabbalat Shabbat*, the evening service with which the holy day began, Reb Sholem Refoelkess went out to talk with the young men who worshipped in the Hasidic synagogue of the Ger dynasty.

"Velvela, Laibushel," he would call out, "come over here a minute. I see that your clothes are getting shorter. 'Modern times,' you'll tell me. But look at my brother Shmuel Laib. Why, he is able to meet with the Czar himself—and he's an observant Jew besides—yet he doesn't cut his sidelocks short, nor his capote. He transacts business with princes and travels abroad. And you? You are already starting to spruce up at the House of Study, in there behind the stove. I'll have you know that as one shortens a little here and a little there, one's fear of God is likewise cut short . . ."

Reb Sholem Refoelkess was in a transport of satisfaction. It wasn't only that he had no regrets over losing the tarpaulin, but also that the *neshamah yetzerah*, the "additional soul" that is said to take possession of a Jew on the Sabbath, radiated cheer within him. He felt the exhilaration of one who has overthrown a powerful enemy. His clothes were dry by this time—it was not at all as though he had so recently been drenched to the skin. He returned home in the rapture of one who, during the festival of Simchat Torah, follows in a winding procession the scrolls of the Law as they are carried through the synagogue; and he chanted the *Sholem Aleichem Malachai Hasheret* with a fervor that Kaila had never seen before.

The same could hardly be said for the deportment of Reb Sholem Refoelkess's competitors in the marketplace. To some degree they invariably transgressed the law of ushering in as well as ushering out the Sabbath. But

Sholem was not concerned about that. He did not rebuke
them, but neither did he give in to their ways. Pausing at
the threshold of the store, he would recall once again the
time when Kaila was preparing for the birth of her first
child. True, he had not amassed any wealth; but he had
brought up a family and kept the Sabbath. And since for
half a century Satan had not been able to ensnare him
into desecrating the Sabbath by tempting him at the
store, it was not likely that such a trap could be laid for
him now.

He left the store and walked over to where a group of
shopkeepers were talking about how the peasants had
become more sophisticated in the ways of merchandis-
ing and were selling their oats directly to the teamsters.
When during the discussion, the matter of the Sabbath
came up. Sholem gestured for them to be silent. Then he
began, addressing no one in particular: "If, God forbid, a
business transaction should lead to the desecration of the
Sabbath, the profit thus gained is insignificant compared
to the wrong that is committed. Indeed, what is there to
be compared to the merit of observing the Sabbath?
Even if one were to acquire a fortune, so long as it
involved desecrating the Sabbath, the result would be a
loss."

The shopkeepers shrugged, wondering who was being
castigated, and why he attached such importance to the
desecration of the Sabbath.

"Reb Sholem, is it for you to see that we observe the
Sabbath?" Bainush the carter wanted to know. "Are you
so untouchable when it comes to desecrating it yourself?"

Pleased by the carter's remark, one by one the shopkeepers sauntered off. Sholem stood there chagrined by
Bainush's impertinence. But soon he regained his composure and his smile returned.

Standing in the doorway of the store, Sholem would watch an approaching customer to see whether he strayed toward another shop. He was aware that if he went away even for a moment, Laizer Avrom was likely to snatch a customer from him.

As he got on in years, Sholem grew indolent; he found it hard to get up early. He could not understand why, more and more, his knees tended to give way and the sacks of oats and bran to become ever more back-breaking. He pondered the question of whether it was time for him to retire. How long ought one to remain in harness? On the other hand, how was he to fare if he gave up his source of income? Would he find himself at the mercy of his children?

The thought that he might, God forbid, have to depend on the children for support in his declining years, won out over his fatigue. As in years past, sacks of oats and bran were piled against the walls of the store; he still wore the same old jackboots and the same greasy, flour-encrusted smock. He remembered hearing his father remark that elderly people preferred to go on doing things in the same old way. Then how could he bear the thought of retiring?

Thinking the whole thing over, Reb Sholem came more and more to cherish his little shop. He envisioned every sack of grain as embodying the blessing of Mother Earth. He was now drawn to the store just as, a newly married man free of financial worries, he had been drawn to the House of Study. Even in his dreams he saw himself busy with peasants and drovers in their sheepskin coats, filling measures of bran and oats and lugging them to the scales. When the dream was over and the peasants had vanished, his eyelids would begin to quiver and he would awaken.

One day Reb Sholem found it harder than ever to get

up. As a ray of light made its way through a crack in the shutters, he pictured himself still filling the teamsters' sacks with oats . . . and anxious to get rid of the customers. He pulled a lean and shrunken hand from underneath the bedclothes and rubbed his eyes, still heavy with sleep. He dreaded having to get out of bed; he would have preferred to turn over and go back to sleep. But a moment later he felt the spur that never failed to drive him on while he was in the store: the thought of Laizer Avrom already standing at the entrance of his own shop, serving all the customers who seemed to come flocking to him. Sholem jumped to his feet, did the ritual ablution of the hands, pulled on his trousers and the flour-encrusted smock, and began to intone the morning prayers. Kaila stirred in her sleep; it seemed to her that Sholem ought not to have awakened so early today. She was about to ask him something or other, but then she dozed off again.

When his morning prayers were over, Sholem filled his big tobacco pipe that resembled the rabbi's pipe shank. He never made a move without that pipe, which was of a sort rarely found in Poland. If it hadn't been for Shmuel Laib, who had brought it as a gift from Prussia, he never would have owned such a thing. When it was lit, he stepped outside. There was a mild breeze, bringing the smell of the pine forest from across the Bug River. Reb Sholem walked with hurried steps along the empty street. A tranquil stillness hung over the houses and the shacks of the poor. His footsteps echoed on the pavement. A dog barked and somewhere a cock began to crow.

He got out the keys that were fastened to his suspenders and unlocked the store, leaving the doors wide open. Once he had put out several half-filled sacks of bran and oats, he stood leaning against the doorpost and looking into the marketplace. He began to be apprehensive about the prevailing silence; he was not accustomed to seeing empty streets and alleys. The familiar marketplace now seemed to him strange and uncanny: no peasant carts loaded with grain and produce, no calves, not a potato in sight. It must still be very early, he thought; he must have gotten up hours ahead of time, even though it seemed to him that he had overslept—but what an eerie silence! It must be that the clock wasn't keeping good time. Reb Sholem was not in the habit of waiting for a customer or a peasant cart to halt near his store. He stepped out, puffing restively at his pipe. Why wasn't the marketplace bustling as usual? How was it that the women vendors hadn't put up their booths and stalls?

"Lord! To have made such a mistake!" he upbraided himself. "I thought it was late—and here the dawn is just breaking. Who knows—perhaps it was all wrong to be praying at such an early hour. But then again, they are likely to show up any minute now," he told himself.

The peasants usually arrived all at once, swarming through the marketplace, unharnessing their nags and turning them around in the shafts so as to face the wagons. Then they would come flocking into his store all at once. But now everything was at a standstill, Kaila still asleep—so how was he to manage, all by himself, on this morning? . . . It could be that he hadn't slept soundly last night; or possibly it was a recurrent backache that had driven him out of bed . . .

Meanwhile, the solemn hush continued. Although the place could turn into a beehive of activity at any moment, the atmosphere just now was becoming ominous. He strained his ears to catch the first creak of a peasant cart, but to no avail. Never once, since he had become a shopkeeper had he gotten up so early. Invariably Laizer Avrom and Mendel Shenker had been there ahead of him . . .

No longer is Reb Sholem concerned with peasant carts hauling sacks of oats that are for sale a little cheaper early in the morning, or with the chore of filling the sacks with bran. He is now anxious just for the sight of a human being. Moments drag past like eternities. He paces up and down in front of his store, intent on the scene about him, hoping to catch sight of anyone whatever. And behold, who should now approach but his brother Shmuel Laib! Sholem shakes his head in amazement. What has brought Shmuel Laib here on a weekday? Throughout the week his brother is usually either en route to Danzig or on his way back. Trembling now, Sholem hastens down the narrow alley, to make quite sure it is Shmuel Laib. And what he sees—or is it an illusion?—is a Shmuel Laib in holiday attire, prayer shawl draped about his shoulders. Now, here comes someone else—it is the shammas, about to pass him by. Pipe still in his mouth, Reb Sholem Refoelkess waits to be greeted with a friendly "Good morning." Instead, the man merely pauses a moment, eyeing Sholem as though he were some weird creature; then he lowers his head and rushes past.

The shammas should be the first to greet him, not the other way around. How is he to account for the man's bad manners? Reb Sholem wonders. Still other Jews now come into sight—yet not a single cart! What's more, he becomes aware that the other Jews are walking at a leisurely pace, without their customary bustle. He still can't account for the shammas's rudeness: not to greet Reb Sholem Refoelkess with a "Good morning!" Giving the shammas a hard look, he concluded that he will settle accounts with him another time. But at the next moment he catches sight of the man accosting several Jews with the outcry, "Look, fellow Jews, at what's happening to Reb Sholem Refoelkess!"

As the townsmen turned around to face Reb Sholem,

the marketplace echoed with the dismaying words, "Reb Sholem, God be with you! What are you doing? A store open for business—a pipe in your mouth! Don't you realize that this is the Sabbath?"

Threatening fists were raised against him, and the words still echoed: "On the Sabbath!" At last, the meaning of what he had done began to dawn on him. Drenched in a frozen sweat of horror, Reb Sholem flung his pipe at the pavement, where it smashed into smithereens, the smoke still rising from its smoldering contents. He wanted to come forward and say something or other to his accusers. But, paralyzed as he was with fear, what felt like a shard of the broken pipe stuck in his throat. Underneath the tobacco-stained gray moustache, his lips began to tremble. But he could not articulate a word. A momentary convulsion went through him, and then he collapsed to the ground.

GRANDMOTHER MIRKA

Winter came early. Shortly after the seasonal rains, freezing weather set in. The carts of dry firewood that the peasants hauled into town were surrounded by anxious customers, and in no time an entire shipment was bought up. An arctic wind blew from the Bug River, chilling people to their bones. The townsmen had not yet put on their winter garb, and anyone who ventured out beat a retreat right away. The water-logged, fertile fields and the black-crested forest urged along the nocturnal gloom, the dense, damp fog, that hovered over the town. An old lady scurried down the slope of a sparsely settled knoll, the wind tearing at her long dress and propelling her forward. The closer she got to the valley, the more the thin ice coating the muggy path snapped under her feet.

Under a veil she clutched an alms box with coins she had collected to be distributed for the Sabbath among the indigent. It was Thursday, and Grandmother Mirka was hurrying home. Tomorrow morning she would make her rounds doling out money to those unable to keep the wolf away from their door.

No one was curious about where Grandmother Mirka came from. The town's graybeards remembered that her father was an observant Jew, a timber merchant whom the landed gentry trusted implicitly, and that her mother was the daughter of a cantor. But even these meager details did not interest anyone. Grandmother Mirka was a person to be reckoned with—a genealogical tree on which burgeoned children and grandchildren. In arranging a marriage, it enhanced one's status to be related to

17

Grandmother Mirka—even to be only a third cousin. She was called affectionately Grandmother Mirka not only by her grandchildren but by the entire community.

She was frail, short, and scrawny and when she stooped, she had all the earmarks of a twelve-year-old girl, bending under her yoke. She was nimble and she never missed a mitzvah dance.* In the women's section of the synagogue she was invariably the first to arrive and the last to leave. Her age was discernible only in the hollows of her cheeks, in which yellow spots had formed, and on the coarse skin of her hands, which performed arduous tasks, such as hauling heavy packs to the marketplace, peeling potatoes, scrubbing pots and pans, and laundering.

Grandmother Mirka lived alone in a small house she had inherited. The door opened onto a huge room, with two windows facing the street and a casement facing the courtyard. The living quarters were white-washed and clean. Across from the door there was a large oven with a broad cornice. In the oven there was a built-in tube in which a tea kettle was placed on the Sabbath. In the winter the warmth generated by the oven spread through the house and the family sat with their backs to it. Near the door there was a broad bench on which rested a water barrel with wide brass hoops. Beside that there was a pail and a copper quart with two handles, and a wooden bucket used to pour the water over one's hands. The floor was fashioned of long, rough-hewn planks; and in the center there was a trapdoor through which one could climb to the cellar. The cellar served as a storehouse for potatoes, beets, carrots, and cabbage. The wall opposite the oak clothes closet was adorned with portraits of rabbis and sages draped in prayer shawls with broad

---

*Dance with the bridegroom and the bride at weddings.

decorated collars. The patriarchal faces with the gray beards and fur-edged hats—worn traditionally by rabbis and Hasidim on festive occasions—gleamed with divine awe. Two Sabbath candlesticks and a massive menorah* rested on a carved chest of drawers.

Grandmother Mirka's kitchen made of whitewashed bricks had chafing dishes and a big oven for roasting. Next to the kitchen there was a small iron stove with long sheet-metal tubes that extended to the chimney. Shortly after the Feast of Tabernacles, when the cold rainy season set in, the little stove was brought into the house. The huge oven reached almost to the ceiling and generated considerable heat but it required dry kindling wood, and about twenty pounds of coal to heat up.

But the most important object in Grandmother Mirka's house was the big grandfather clock with the long pendulum and the yellow dial, on which one could still read the word "Paris." It was in a polished cabinet and needed two keys to wind it. On winter days, when the air was humid, the clock stopped. Grandmother Mirka never took it to a watchmaker. Instead, she dipped a goose feather into petroleum, greased all the wheels, moved the pendulum and—lo and behold—the clock started.

The small house was in a row of dwellings on a slope leading down to the Bug River. Grandmother Mirka was fond of the river. In the summer she looked at the yellowish stream for a long time. In her youth she used to stroll along the beach and on Sabbath afternoons she rowed a boat on the river. She ate the fish from the river for an untold number of years. She remembered the times when the Bug River went on a rampage, inundated villages in the valley, and caused wretchedness and deprivation. Yet no one held a grudge against it.

---

*A candelabrum with seven candlesticks.

In the winter the entire row of houses in Grandmother Mirka's alleyway was snow-covered. The windows were frozen. Long icicles, like tallow candles, dangled from the roof. Dark thick smoke billowed from the chimneys. Iron stoves glowed in the houses and frost-embroidered flowers were visible on the storm windows. Then one day the frozen surface of the river cracked and the melting snow swelled the dormant stream.

Grandmother Mirka was just as agile during the winter as she was the rest of the year. During the day she made the rounds of the town searching for a livelihood. She was always in a hurry, mumbling under her breath, "The day is short and I still have to be here and there." She went home at night, removed her woolen kerchief, the bonnet and the weatherworn coat. She made a fire in the little iron stove, to warm up the house for Shloimala's homecoming (the big oven would take much longer to generate heat).

When the little stove burned red and the house heated up, Grandmother Mirka's cheeks flushed like tomatoes in the blazing sun. She no longer felt weary from the day's hustle, she cherished the crooked, coarse little cottage as a veritable mansion.

"Well, are we not to thank the Everlasting One," she said to Shloimala when he returned. "Poor people are roaming the highways; artisans and tradesmen still trudge along wearily on their way home. So when you find yourself in such a warm, cozy atmosphere, and there is no shortage of potatoes, then you must not sin."

Squatting on a stool, she peeled the potatoes skillfully. During the winter she peeled more than enough potatoes for two people. She cooked a big pot of barley soup, spiking it with onions and goose cracklings and well-browned roasted bits of goose skin. She served Shloimala the first bowl.

At night, pricking her ears up at the slightest noise, she urged him to be quiet. "Ha! I think someone is around his way outside the window. Open the door—maybe someone is trying to come in."

Occasionally an impoverished Jew, wandering from town to town, dropped in. She looked forward to such times. And when a visitor, hungry and chilled to the bone, appeared, Grandmother Mirka welcomed him with open arms, saying, "Please sit down in this chair, near the little stove, so your frozen beard will thaw. Take off your coat. Soon the oven will be warm, too. Meanwhile, have a glass of tea."

The next moment she gave the guest a glass of hot tea and poppyseed cookies. And when he started to cough she urged him to try her own remedy.

"I see that you have a slight cold," she went on. "I will brew a special drink for you. Have you said your afternoon prayers yet? I'll have dinner ready soon."

But after the evening meal, when the guest lingered near the oven, she became a bit apprehensive. She was distressed that she could not carry out the *mitzvah* of hospitality in full. Since she had become a widow, she wanted to avoid malicious gossip, and so no strange man could stay overnight in her home. When the visitor dozed off, she let him sleep an hour or two, whereupon she woke him up and said, "Reb Yid, here are a few pieces of rock candy that will relieve your cough at night." That was a hint that it was getting late—and that it was improper for a stranger to remain with her alone.

On Sabbath afternoons Grandmother Mirka was champing at the bit to have a guest at her table. Freezing weather and knee-deep snow could not deter her from attending the Sabbath service in the synagogue. She acted as the *zogarin*, the one who intoned the prayers in the women's section and the illiterate women repeated after her. But during the winter months the women's section was almost deserted, and Grandmother Mirka prayed by herself. When she left the synagogue and saw someone who was not invited anywhere for a Sabbath meal, she wanted to invite him herself, but she could never bring herself to do so. How would it look to be accompanied home by a stranger, she reflected. But it was something else again when such a guest came of his own volition. She did not ask who sent him or how he learned that she received guests. She had an inkling that it was the doing of Hershel the sexton. He used to direct such guests to hosts where he knew they would find a sumptuous meal.

SABBATH

Throughout the week Grandmother Mirka had her hands full, looking after her own as well as communal affairs. But on the Sabbath she blossomed and the women thought it was as though the Divine Presence hovered over her. She seemed to grow younger and Friday, at twilight, she looked forward ardently to the coming of the Sabbath as if it were a queen. She was most careful not to be tardy with the ceremony of lighting the Sabbath candles—particularly so on Short Friday. She lit the candles in the antiquated brass candlesticks handed down through the last three generations.

Shloimala was never late for his mother's lighting the Sabbath candles. But Grandmother Mirka clung to the tradition of having two grandchildren or great-grandchildren present during the ceremony. She lingered over this ritual, covering her eyes with both hands. Her lips trembled and not a sound came out of her mouth. And when a grandchild asked, "Grandma, why did you stand so long with your eyes covered?" she would answer amicably, "While I'm lighting the candles I can have whatever I want by praying. And I must keep everybody in mind: your fathers and mothers and you—*all of you!* And you, darling," she addressed a little granddaughter, and lifted the child's chin, "should know that lighting candles is one of the three commandments imposed upon women. And when you grow up, you should observe these commandments, whatever may happen."

With the inauguration of the Sabbath, Grandmother

Mirka put on her best festive clothes. First she took out the silk dress with the long tassels and white embroidered cuffs around her hands. As she strode in her ample, pleated dress, the silk rustled. The gown was adorned with a wide embroidered collar with little straps. And she flaunted a string of pearls which she kept hidden so that no grandchild could lay hands on it.

She walked to the synagogue with delicate steps, proudly, with dignity and ease. In her Sabbath headgear she appeared much taller. In the women's section of the synagogue she had a seat near the east wall—a location reserved for the privileged. But she frequently stood at the door among the women who could not pay for a pew, because she had relinquished her seat to a frail woman or to an expectant mother.

Grandmother Mirka did not wear all the jewelry that she possessed. Only once a year did she put on all her finery: it was the second day of Rosh Hashanah. On that occasion she spruced up like an affluent woman. She put on a long brooch with gold rings, a long massive chain with a double-case watch at its end, diamond earrings set in platinum, and gold bracelets on her wrists. In one hand she clutched an heirloom prayerbook for the Jewish holidays in silver covers. And when an impertinent grandchild asked, "Grandmother, why did you get all dolled up?" she answered quietly and piously, "Today, on the second day of Rosh Hashanah, benedictions on all kinds of food are being distributed for the entire year. And one is rewarded in accordance with the appearance one makes: thus, a poor man is allotted a hundred and fifty roubles, on which he has to subsist a whole year, whereas a wealthy woman commands a little more respect. You are judged by what you show."

On Rosh Hashanah, Grandmother Mirka proceeded early to the synagogue, where she sat in her reserved pew, yielding it to no one. She intoned the prayers from the book with the silver-plated covers, occasionally letting the tears stream down her face, until she returned home convinced of one thing: that she had secured a livelihood for the coming year through prayer. As to keeping your nose to the grindstone—well, you can't sit around twiddling your thumbs throughout the year.

Grandmother Mirka was a skilled baker and cook and her culinary art was highly praised by the community. Her Sabbath *kugel* was especially extolled. If someone wished to praise a certain dish, he would say, "It is as delicious as Grandmother Mirka's *kugel*. For the Sabbath she prepared a special menu: *tcholent*, a baked dish of meat, potatoes and legumes, in saturated fat, dark-brown potatoes like moist dates, and rice *kugel* with cinnamon. Grandmother Mirka only rarely indulged in making a rice *kugel*, but especially on the Sabbath following Passover. She kept Simchat Torah apples and black walnuts in store. The get-together continued until nightfall. People recapitulated and commented upon all the events that occurred in the community during the preceding week.

THE DEAF-MUTE GUTCHELA

On the Sabbath and on other holidays Grandmother Mirka was preoccupied with herself and with her immediate family. But on weekdays she cared for the community. She lent a helping hand to those who lived from hand to mouth and visited the sick, and the Yeshivah students who had to be provided with meals and lodging. And when the marriage of a poor bridegroom had to be financed, she knew whom to approach for contributions. Many indigent townsmen called on her for assistance, and she always responded with a comforting word or advice. But it was the mute Gutchela on whom she lavished most of her attention.

"Everyone else is able to talk, to cry and protest, but she can't express herself, for God has rendered her a deaf-mute," Grandmother Mirka used to say.

Gutchela is still beautiful, but years ago she was gorgeous. Her blond tresses flashed like sunlight. Tall, stately, as if she were sculpted by a master, she had glowing blue eyes and lips like ripe cherries. Her misfortune was that she was a deaf mute! And this calamity led to another, even worse: once at twilight some Gentile boys trapped her under the bridge by sprinkling caramels and rabbit nuts in front of her. She fought back but could not scream for help. When they released her she ran to her Uncle Menashe's home where she was given a bunk. She was bruised, traumatized and pale as a ghost—but inarticulate, as usual. There was some talk about marrying her to Sholinger's oldest son, whose head was a bit askew, and whose right hand shook with palsy. But when he heard the malicious gossip about her, even this cripple turned away. So she remained a spinster—luckily without a bastard.

Grandmother Mirka was the only one to whom she ever applied for help. She never looked anyone straight in the eye. When she was at her wits' end, she went to Grandmother Mirka's and paused in the doorway, looking at the old woman with sad and imploring eyes. When Grandmother Mirka saw these eyes, she could tell that the girl was hungry, or that her uncle had put her bunk out in the courtyard, or that she needed an old nightgown. The deaf-mute was always welcomed with patience and consideration, and she never left emptyhanded.

GRANDMOTHER MIRKA'S FASTS

Though slight and scrawny she was never sick, and when she was indisposed, she refused to visit a doctor. "What can they do for me in my old age?" she asked. "God is a Father. If I am to recover it will be the will of the Everlasting One."

But it was a different story when others were ailing. If someone destitute was stricken, she went out of her way to help. For the sick and infirm that coughed, she brought jars of jam, reserving this delicacy especially for pregnant women. Her panacea for every affliction was fasting. A visit to the sick was not an ordinary visit. She preceded it by fasting on a Monday or a Thursday. "Even though the doctor prescribes medicine," she argued, "he desecrates the Sabbath, and God pays more attention to those who serve Him."

As Grandmother Mirka grew older, her children and grandchildren urged her to give up making the rounds on Thursdays in inclement weather, collecting alms and twisted white loaves for the Sabbath of the indigent; and to stop fasting. It was not easy to persuade her to give up the first of these duties; but the task was almost insurmountable on the second. She would not forgo any of the five traditional fast-days: Tishah b'Av, the Fast of Gedaliah, the Day of Atonement, the Fast of Esther, and the Fast of the First-born. She would not renounce any of her self-imposed fasts. Thursday was the most formidable day. She fasted and made the rounds with the alms box.

"Mother, you ought to eat something," Leah, her oldest daughter, pleaded with her to no avail.

"Mirka, when you perform a *mitzvah*, a good deed—making the rounds with the alms box in freezing weather—the great commandment of *tzodoka*, charity—you are absolved of the duty of fasting. Indeed, Heaven does not request twofold observance from you," Uncle Leuben argued with her.

"It doesn't matter—God will give me strength," she replied. And she continued in her ways.

If a member of the family took sick, she added a fast-day to her schedule. She insisted that a lot can be accomplished by fasting. And if someone tried to challenge that conviction, she lost no time in advancing her ironclad evidence: "What would have happened if Mordecai and the Righteous Queen Esther had not fasted for three days? Would even a single Jew have survived in the Susa capital?"

Once, in her declining years, one of her great-grandchildren fell ill. The doctor diagnosed the ailment as rather serious and ordered that the medication be scrupulously administered. Aware of the ominous situation, Grandmother Mirka hastened to supplement her own cure-all, an extra fast-day. And she made a vow to the Everlasting One that if the child recovered, she would increase the number of her fast-days. And—lo and behold! God helped. And Grandmother Mirka, God forbid, did not default.

SHLOIMALA

There came a time when Grandmother Mirka had only one son named Shloimala left in her house. He was haggard, gaunt and pale. He was sick most of his life, with a hacking cough. He spent his days poring over the Talmudic folios in the House of Study. Grandmother Mirka guarded him like the apple of her eye. He tried various herb concoctions and amulets and good-luck charms, yet could not shake off the cough. But when the condition deteriorated and he had attacks of choking and suffocating, his mother decided to consult a prominent physician. The latter examined the patient and diagnosed the situation as hopeless. But Grandmother Mirka did not lose heart. Spurning the doctor's verdict, she resorted to her own methods. She started the regimen by feeding him a glass of milk with honey in the morning. There followed a "guggle muggle"—a concoction of egg yolk, butter, and sugar, and a lamb chop or a fat pullet. "Shloimala, please do it for me—eat this chicken leg, and you'll be able to pronounce the proper benediction," she pleaded.

As Shloimala grew, she begrudged herself looking at him. He rolled his sidelocks behind his ears. He sprouted a thick moustache, his narrow shoulders broadened, and his mother beamed with joy. But it disconcerted her that he was inclined to take the law into his own hands. For instance, he grabbed Laibush the carter's whip and chased the goats all over the marketplace, or ran wild with the youngsters, hid his ritual fringes in his trousers, contrary to tradition. Grandmother Mirka recalled that she was in agony while she was pregnant with Shloimala. Everybody predicted that she would give birth to a girl. When she heard that, she spat three times, then she hastened to the women's section of the synagogue, where she implored the Lord—she refused to divulge the nature of her prayer to anyone—to take pity on her so that she might give birth to a male child. As time went on, she was more sure that it was a boy. Her belly was pointed and the fetus inside kicked up a row.

"Can such a puny woman give birth to a boy?" Women whispered to one another.

And Grandmother Mirka did give birth to a boy and named him Shloimala. The infant dropped into the world like the fear of God that goes with the Eighteen Benedictions: stock-still and without a squawk. In order to make him breathe he had to be smacked on the buttocks and heaved up and down. When that wasn't enough, two washtubs, one filled with cold water, the other with warm, were brought in, and the child was immersed, now in one, now in the other. Then its temples were massaged with lemon, until it let out a cry. He cried out and tackled his mother's breast and wouldn't let go, that's how hungry he was.

When Shloimala arrived, Grandmother Mirka was excited. She was aware of one thing: she had a son!

Whatever children's diseases were going around—measles, "the English ailment," chickenpox, a bloated belly, inflamed tonsils—this infant was sure to be afflicted with it. She consulted a physician or an elderly peasant from a nearby village who was reputed to be a "healer of all flesh." Sometimes she resorted to conjuring an evil eye. However, when the situation deteriorated, when the child ran a high temperature and did not open his eyes, Grandmother Mirka resorted to fasting on two or three occasions—and the patient recovered!

When illness struck outside the immediate family, she was the virtuoso. First of all, she didn't tremble as much as when Shloimala fell ill. Grandmother Mirka was good at taking anyone's pulse and gauging his temperature by placing her hand on the patient's forehead. She asked about the condition of the abdomen, she recommended a diet, stressing the need to drink a lot of water in certain instances. At other times, a glass of camomile, special herbs, salves and lotions and, sometimes, she recommended the application of leeches.

As Shloimala grew, she used him to help haul her wares and her loaded wicker baskets to the marketplace, while she made the rounds of individual homes. But she could never think of making a businessman of him. Shloimala had to study the Law and serve God. Each modicum of the Torah that he studied, each verse of Holy Writ that he articulated, every page of the Talmud that he intoned—was worth vastly more than all the baskets of haberdashery that she had and the profits she derived from them. She tried to manage somehow, but under no circumstances did she deprive Shloimala even of one hour in the House of Study.

As Shloimala grew up, he took to reading forbidden, secular books that he secured outside the House of Study, without his mother's knowledge. Those books served to introduce him to another world.

One winter Shloimala tried to climb into a sleigh driven by some playful neighborhood boys and girls of his age. Carefree he tried to grab the little pole but missed his footing and fell flat on his face. Cold compresses with vinegar had to be applied to his bruised and swollen face and nose throughout the night. Grandmother Mirka knew that it was retribution for distracting his attention from the study of the Torah, but she did not rebuke Shloimala.

She assumed that he would never again run after tinkling horse-drawn sleighs. But that's not what happened. If anything, his preference for ice skating and sledding grew. Grandmother Mirka did everything in her power to dissuade him from that sport and urged him to take care of his health. She even bought new boots for him and pleaded with him not to ruin them by skating. They went on like this for a while. But when his health deteriorated and the hacking cough got worse, his face flushed and he gasped for air, he stopped the sledding and skating and resumed the study of the Gemara in the warm House of Study.

GRANDMOTHER MIRKA'S GRANDCHILDREN

Even with all her communal responsibilities Grandmother Mirka remained devoted to her grandchildren and great-grandchildren. With the impending winter, she knitted long woolen stockings and woolen gloves for the girls, and scarfs for the boys and a bag for the phylacteries for the Bar Mitzvah. The girls grew by leaps and bounds. They married fine young men from other towns, had children and their share of joys and tribulations, and in due time became almost oblivious of the town. The only person they were close to was Grandmother Mirka. They inquired about her from visiting townsmen and always sent their regards. There wasn't a thing they wouldn't do for her. They all penned letters to her but she didn't engage in correspondence, and her relatives were at a loss to fathom her reason for not writing.

Grandmother Mirka read the letters, and she responded by sending regards with functionaries who made the rounds of the neighboring towns. She had no patience for writing, finding someone to address the envelope in Russian, or looking for a postage stamp. "What's the use scribbling on a piece of paper?" she asked. "What a man doesn't hear with his own ears doesn't get into his heart."

GRANDMOTHER MIRKA'S INSURRECTION STORIES

More than anything else, Grandmother Mirka liked to tell stories. In the winter, when the landscape was frozen solid and pedestrians were chilled to the bones, and their teeth chattered, and the arctic blasts penetrated every nook and cranny—she filled the extra bright lamp with kerosene, with her back hugging the warm wall of the tile oven, and launched into her narratives, which she delivered like choice morsels. The house gradually filled up with visitors: an aunt, an uncle, neighbors, who sat down in a semicircle. Grandmother Mirka signaled the listeners to cease their chatter, and proceeded. Everyone fell silent, including a dignified relative with a patriarchal beard.

The stories were unique. They dealt neither with phantoms and apparitions nor with rabbis, or the Garden of Eden, or the wicked who boil in casks of pitch in the infernal regions of Gehenna. She recounted events that she herself had experienced. Especially indelible and crystal clear in her memory was the great miracle that concerned Shloimala during the Polish insurrection.

"None of you had been born yet at that time," she began, "when the Poles rebelled, resorted to lese majesty, and attempted to overthrow the Czar's dominion of their homeland. Alexander II reigned then, and it was reported that he was a more liberal monarch than his father, Nicholas I. But the moment he ascended the throne he

35

began to persecute the Poles. They retaliated by staging huge protest demonstrations in Warsaw three years before the mutiny.

Czar Alexander II promulgated a decree to have the insurgents penalized. The ferocious Cossacks charged into the masses, wielding their swords ruthlessly. And when the Czar ordered the conscription of all twenty-one-year-old Poles into the Russian armed forces, the move infuriated the Polish nation even more, and helped trigger the Polish insurrection.

"As an opening move, thousands of young Poles went underground in the primeval forests, from where they waged a guerrilla war against the Russians. Then they organized an entire army and battled the Cossacks on a grand scale. Alexander entered into a compact with Germany: Bismarck, the Iron Chancellor, agreed not to violate the Russo-German western frontier as long as the Russo-Polish hostilities continued. Alexander II then pulled the Cossack Corps away from that border and deployed it in Poland. The Muscovites went on a rampage, slaughtering the people and razing the gentry's estates to the ground. The leaders of the insurrection were hung. At times whole rows of mutineers were strung up on poplar trees. But the Polish patriots, armed with rifles and bayonets and led by Polish noblemen, fought gallantly. Entire detachments bivouacked and trained on the estates of the landed proprietors from where they proceeded to the battlefield. They generally marched through the town at dawn, rousing the townsmen with the singing of their national anthem. *Jeszcze Polska nie zginela*—Poland still is ours forever, as long as Poles remain. People queued up to watch the procession. Old peasants burst into tears. Russian gendarmes ran for cover.

"Not just Poles, Jews also joined the Polish insurrection. For instance, I knew Yossele the glazier. He wore a Polish army uniform with the four-corner headgear, and he marched along in the same platoon. The Poles let him carry the Polish flag. He went into combat with them.

"The insurgents were in the good graces of our community. But once, at nightfall, the Cossacks raided our town, running riot, lashing out at young and old, Gentile and Jew, with their cat-o'-nine-tails. Pandemonium set in. The streets were deserted as the populace ran for cover. The Cossacks invaded the homes, pillaging, murdering, raping. When dusk mercifully set in, I grabbed Shloimala—he was still a child—and hastened to the cemetery, where we hid among the gravestones. We crouched there in mortal fear for a day and two nights. Returning home we found everything in disarray. Luckily, the jewelry and the candlesticks were concealed in the cellar and escaped the greed of the marauders."

Grandmother Mirka took a breathing spell and a sip of water, then resumed her reminiscences:

"There was a running battle between the insurgents and the Cossacks not far from our town. The Poles lay in a line on the ground and directed a fusillade at the Cossacks, killing many. But before long the Russians closed ranks again and, screaming 'Hurrah!' galloped down the hill on their fiery steeds, brandishing gleaming swords, charging into the midst of the Polish patriots. The carnage that ensued was terrible. Heads rolled, bodies were mutilated, horses' entrails were spilled, men and beasts were jumbled in a bloody mass. After the Cossacks got reinforcements and occupied the villages along with the lordly manors, they continued their orgy of blood, sending anyone who happened to be in their way to kingdom come.

"The police, once again, came into sight in town. They accompanied the Cossack patrols at night, abducting the

Poles from their homes and exiling them to Siberia for penal servitude. The Russian forces of occupation then abolished Polish legal authority. The use of the Polish language in administrative offices was rescinded. Russian became the official tongue. And the landed gentry who supported the uprising were deprived of their lands and goods, which were distributed among the peasants."

THE RED ROOSTER IS THE FIRST TO CROW

In Nissan,* when the community was making preparations for the coming holiday, Grandmother Mirka suddenly mumbled to herself, "It isn't worth the time! . . ."

On being asked for an explanation of her words, she answered ambiguously, "The red rooster is the first to crow every day. Dark, ill-omened clouds loom above. The rivers will run red . . ."

The relatives understood that Grandmother Mirka was deviating from her traditional ways. She gave up fasting. She no longer made the rounds collecting alms, and became apathetic toward her grandchildren. She took to bed ominously, asked for some water to make her ablutions, and asked that someone recite with her the *Shema.* She asked the assembled old women if everything was in readiness. Then she turned to face the wall—and was joined to her ancestors.

Uncle Reuben, who was present, observed fervently, "She was a righteous woman. She died like a saint."

It was only on Tishah b'Av, a day of mourning in commemoration of the destruction of the First and Second Temples of Jerusalem, at the outbreak of the First World War, that people came to understand what Grandmother Mirka meant by the crowing of the red rooster and the looming dark clouds. To endure a war would have been too much for her.

*The seventh month in the Jewish calendar, coinciding with parts of March and April.

Some elderly women envied her. They knew that she would be spared the *hibut ha'Kever*—in Jewish lore, the distress of a wrongdoer in his grave. She was welcomed to the Garden of Eden forthwith.

Grandmother Mirka was the talk of the community—as a wise and saintly woman.

MY GRANDFATHER'S MELAVEH MALKAH*

1

My grandfather, Shmuel Laib, was seventy years old but in good health and as sturdy as an oak. His children were married, and he and Grandmother spent their declining years alone.

He had a powerful physique, a bony face, a long beard and a moustache streaked with gray. He walked as straight as an arrow, recognized people from far away, and still had his good hearing.

It was obvious that he was a tower of strength in his youth. He grew up in the great outdoors, between town and village, in the meadows and forests. In the course of many years, he supervised the peasants who felled and hauled the timber to the Bug River.

Grandfather drove to the forest like a member of the gentry in a coach drawn by two chestnut horses, and driven by a coachman.

When he arrived in the forest, the work of the rangers and lumberjacks was already in full swing. He would take in at a glance the number of logs and the "quarters" of timber that had been piled up. He stepped lively among the clusters of trees, making notes, then returning to the lumberjacks.

Grandfather did not put on airs. He was on good terms with the common laborer. Now and then, he would treat them to a pack of shag tobacco and cigarette paper, and a big bottle of hard liquor in freezing weather.

---

*"The ushering out of the queen"—the evening meal marking the conclusion of the Sabbath.

Grandfather Shmuel Laib also liked manual labor. And when the workers struggled with a particularly heavy log, he hoisted it onto the lorry by himself.

After grandfather left the forest, the lumberjacks took a break, lit up, and one of them said, "What a Jew! The strength the man has! The three of us fell flat on our faces while he, all by himself, heaved the beam as though it were a spindle."

"He's as strong as ten beasts of burden," another observed.

"No wonder—he eats white bread and roast goose."

"And yet he was never drafted."

"Because Czar Nicholas does not like Jewish soldiers."

"Who said that the Czar does not like Jewish soldiers? Wasn't Moshek a 'Nikolayevsky soldier'?* And didn't Abram Kravietz serve the entire hitch?"

"What's the reason, then?"

"He wasn't conscripted because he is a merchant of the first guild."

"That is right!" the elderly Anton commented. "Merchants of the first guild are exempt, while peasants are conscripted for twenty-five years and are banished to Harbin."

2

Grandfather relished space. The time he spent in the forests and on the estates of the gentry had instilled in him a craving for the space the affluent were used to. In his house there were two big rooms to accommodate large parties of guests. The house was made of wood but

---

*In Czarist Russia, in the nineteenth century, Jewish children—some as young as ten years—were conscripted into the armed forces for a period of twenty-five years and banished to Siberia, where most were converted to Christianity and many died of the hardships.

constructed massively. It had small porches and an anteroom between the kitchen and the courtyard, where there was a private well with a long bucket. The house was furnished with oak closets and massive carved tables. Large tile ovens with big cornices provided heat during the winter months. At one time, Jews were afraid to pass through that area at night. But Grandfather Shmuel Laib was dauntless in his youth. He settled there and was the only Jewish resident for a long time. Years later Jewish neighbors came to live there.

Even in his declining years, Grandfather was not idle. Although he no longer engaged in large business ventures, such as buying up sprawling forests and felling their timber, he still dispatched rafts to Danzig. When he retired from work in the forest, he devoted himself to reciting Psalms and to the study of one page of the Talmud each day.

In the evening, holding a lantern that he guarded like the apple of his eye, he made his way to the small Hasidic house of prayer of the Ger dynasty known as the *shtibbel*. The little synagogue was situated on a predominantly Gentile street, where dogs ran out and barked and growled, but this never irked him.

He concerned himself with the people of the town. Thus, he never smiled at the nouveau riche, but when some rich man became impoverished, Grandfather extended him a helping hand.

Once, grandfather learned that Shaiyela "Nogid"* had been postponing the marriage of his daughter for two years because he could not deliver the substantial dowry that he had promised. Grandfather thought about helping the man without humiliating him. He invited him and said, "As you know, Shaiyela, I never wanted a

---

*Man of wealth

partner. God decides what is to be. Why have two pairs of hands? But now, in my old age—"

"Reb Shmuel Laib, how can you talk about old age? Who can ever say that you're old? I wish I looked as young as you."

"But I am seventy years old, nonetheless. I find it difficult to do things now, and I am looking for a partner—not a full-fledged one, just someone to supervise a few rafts to Danzig."

"Reb Shmuel Laib, I don't have the slightest knowledge about the handling of rafts. I know very little about timber."

"In commercial affairs you can rely on me. I need someone only to keep an eye on hauling the timber from the forest to the river. Someone dependable."

"Is there a shortage of honest people in our community, Reb Shmuel Laib?"

"Do you think it beneath your dignity to go into partnership with me?" Grandfather asked, a bit irritated. "Maybe you think you're richer than I am? But I heard that you are giving your daughter a substantial dowry."

"Of course. She is an only child."

"Well, did you do it?"

Reb Shaiyela blushed. He suddenly realized why his host had invited him.

"I accept, Reb Shmuel Laib," Reb Shaiyela blurted out. "You know what you are doing. As a matter of fact, I do need help."

Grandfather opened the drawer of the massive dresser, took notes and keys out of it, handed them to Shaiyela, and said, "Starting tomorrow, God willing, you will be my partner. Pray with the first *minyan*, and go down to the river. Count the logs the peasants deliver. And I will be there soon after that and give you further instructions."

The rafts were fastened together and made ready for the trip to Danzig. Grandfather sent Shaiyela to collect the money. When he returned they sat down to settle the account. The "partner's" share amounted to a few hundred roubles, and he was paid immediately.

Once a year, grandfather celebrated a *melaveh malkah* in a grand manner. After the *havdalah*, a blessing recited at the termination of the Sabbath, he proceeded to chant special *zemirot—melaveh malkah* hymns.* Grandmother, joined by the servants, got busy in the kitchen. The chafing dishes soon began to glow, and the wide plates were soon crowded with huge pans and pots, in the biggest of which they stewed oatmeal and marrow bones. For the annual *melaveh malkah* festival, Grandmother Mirka enlisted the help of the servants of the entire *mishpachah*, who cooperated in preparing the noodles and peeling potatoes. Now and then, when grandmother stepped outside for a few moments, she exhorted the help to see to it "it should not boil over." The maid-servants tried to outdo one another, so that Reb Shmuel Laib's wife should know who was the best worker. Before long, the smell of the roast drifted out onto the street and teased the passers-by.

The *melaveh malkah* was a feast for the poverty-stricken, who looked forward to that event with bated breath. In addition to the local participants, the indigent from adjacent towns also came.

In the spacious front room, where the windows faced the street, there were long tables covered with white tablecloths reserved for the town's dignitaries. Grand-

---

*The hymn *Eliyahu ha-Navi* (Elijah the Prophet) was of special significance.

mother decorated the tables with her heirloom silver candlesticks. The big candelabra and the spice box rested in the center. The candles radiated a rosy light. There were silver goblets, chalices, and ornate china. The *melavah malkah* festival was like a wedding in an affluent family.

Local scholars, dignitaries and their relatives gathered to pay tribute to Grandfather on that solemn occasion. The guests wore festive attire. The women flaunted their precious brooches, diamond earrings and long gold chains. Their silk-pleated dresses, reaching their ankles, rustled with every move. The women held up the back of their dresses with one hand as they walked. The long sleeves of their garments were closed at their wrists where white embroidered cuffs hid their hands. Some women wore white, brown, and black hats decorated with ribbons, while the affluent young wore wigs so well made that it was impossible to distinguish them from real hair.

Grandfather appeared in his best clothes, the new satin gabardine worn by Orthodox Jews, a freshly laundered shirt, trousers with thin white stripes, chamois boots, and a wide, fine-spun cap. Grandfather himself welcomed the guests, since Grandmother was preoccupied with all sorts of chores in the kitchen. He greeted everyone cordially with a smile, or by offering them a pinch of snuff. He asked the elderly women about the grandchildren and now and then wished them a belated *mazol tov*.

When the guests had washed their hands—a prerequisite of the feast—and were seated, Grandfather stood up to address the guests.

"Even though there are scholarly and erudite guests here," he commenced, "and although you have heard more than once about the miracle that happened to me once at the end of the Sabbath, I want to tell you the story again."

His children and grandchildren knew that when grandfather launched into this reminiscence during the *melaveh malkah*, they had to stand near him.

"Almost fifty years ago, I had to fulfill my military obligation to the Czar," he said. "I thought, of course I have to serve the Czar. I would not rebel against the government, God forbid. But when I gave the matter some thought, I got scared: to spend twenty-five years in a Gentile environment, to eat non-*kosher* food, and to pray without phylacteries. If it were only five years! But twenty-five! Why, that meant I couldn't marry, have children, grandchildren—these generations here." Grandfather gestured toward his descendants.

"Shmuel Laib, chop off two fingers and be done with it," some people advised me. "Well, yes, that sounds logical. It's worth the sacrifice, I thought for a moment. But when I fell asleep, the two fingers that I wanted to chop off confronted me and took me to task: 'What sin have we committed,' they remonstrated. 'How have we wronged you that you should cut us off? We give strength to your hands, we help you to write. We turn the pages in the prayer book and in the Gemara folio for you. Why don't you leave us alone? You ought to cut off a couple of toes. You don't wash them before you eat. You don't need them to count your money. You can't use them to play the violin. And they must not touch the Holy Book.'

"When I woke up, I realized that this was not an ordinary dream. I thought about it, then I said to myself, 'Very well, I'll chop off a part of one leg.' But since it was the eve of the Sabbath, I decided to wait until Sunday.

"That night, when I fell asleep, I was unable to turn over: my feet were numb. Something trampled me and choked me. 'Shmuel Laib, why are you so cruel? What

did we do to deserve such a fate? Didn't we carry you to
the House of Study in freezing weather? Didn't we carry
you to *Selihot** and to *Tashlikh?*† We warn you, we'll get
you! Don't touch us. I, the right foot have agreed with the
left foot that if you dare harm us, we'll refuse to carry
you. You'll have to drag yourself on crutches. You'd
better gouge out one of your eyes, one will do. And it's
easy: All you need is a needle.'

"When I woke up, I was drenched with sweat, that's
how tired my feet had made me. To be spoken to like that,
to have someone shake a fist at you like that—why, that's
no laughing matter. At night, I couldn't move my legs.
My fingers, which I wash before each meal, spoke gently,
but my feet, which sweat in the summer and get stuck in
the muck and mire in the winter, are arrogant. They
immediately threaten you 'You'll need crutches.'

"But what's right is right: you can get by with one eye,
and as long as you live like other Jews, and have a wife
who gives birth to another generation. But which eye
should I lose?"

"So I started to experiment. I closed one eye, then the
other. They were both perfect. But which one was I to
gouge? Which one to spare?

"I was on the horns of this dilemma until I made up my
mind. Come what may, I will serve in Czar Nicholas's
army!

"But when I was all but ready to accept the fateful
sentence, and my mother had packed a few of my
belongings, including phylacteries, a miracle occurred!
In the Sabbath twilight, while I took part in my father's
melaveh malkah—which was supposed to be my last
one—mail arrived from the provincial capital, bearing

Selihot—penitential prayers.
†*Tashlikh*—ceremony held near a running stream. The term derives from
Micah: "Thou wilt cast all their sins into the depths of the sea."

the news that the draft board had drawn lots, and that I was the only one to be exempted from military service!

"Father said, 'Shmuel Laib, the *melaveh malkah* is yours. You've been exempted, because of its merit.'

"And now, my dear friends, eat and drink to your heart's content, and rejoice!"

REB BERELEH

He was called Bereleh. This name hardly fit his figure, broad-shouldered, stalwart, with huge hands that had little cushions, in which pits appeared when the fingers were bent. The hair in his beard was sparse. His feet were sturdy, and his belly was like a barrel.

In spite of his figure, he was agile, and took rapid strides; as he walked almost ran. He managed his affairs alone. He did not trust anyone.

Reb Bereleh's house was open to businessmen and Hasidim. He had inherited his wealth from his parents and from his wife's family. Along with the money he had inherited the responsibility to be generously hospitable and to dispense charity, in keeping with the tradition of his parents and grandparents.

In the *shtibbel* of the Ger Hasidim, Reb Bereleh was the be-all and end-all. And although he had never set his heart on becoming a *gabbai*, or warden, of the little synagogue, no move was made without consulting him. Reb Bereleh had his pew at the east wall, where the highly privileged sat, and it was a time-honored tradition that the congregation did not intone the loud Eighteen Benedictions until Reb Bereleh had completed reciting the silent one.

With the exception of the Rejoicing of the Torah festival, when he remained at home, Reb Bereleh visited the Rabbi of Ger on all holidays, and on those pilgrimages he was invariably accompanied by several poor Hasidim, whose trips he subsidized.

Reb Bereleh was known as a kind soul. His purse was

never inaccessible to the indigent. Whether it was a matter of visiting the sick, or the community's philanthropic service, or marrying off an orphaned or destitute girl, or other such good deeds, Reb Bereleh was the first to contribute, and he urged others to do likewise.

Reb Bereleh's major accomplishment was the establishment of a poorhouse for the impoverished. No one was surprised by Reb Bereleh's generosity. It was common knowledge that he was wallowing in wealth, rich as Croesus. He owned houses and other properties, and he was the banker who supplied the local gentry with loans. It was rumored that he was even a silent partner in the local liquor distilleries.

As far as appearances go, Reb Bereleh had a dry goods store, which his wife Pearl managed. He didn't meddle in this business. She was so preoccupied with the duties and responsibilities of the store that she was hardly at home during the day, with the exception of the Sabbath and festivals.

Reb Bereleh donated to charity not because he was asked to do so, or because it would have been unbecoming for him to withhold a donation; he simply rejoiced in helping his fellow men, especially when an emissary came from another town, or when a needy Talmudic scholar arrived. In such instances Reb Bereleh did not wait until the petitioner had applied to him. He went to visit the newcomer.

Pearl, Reb Bereleh's wife, was also well thought of in the community. She changed maidservants frequently. She frowned upon one girl's behavior, or disapproved of the way another girl washed the dishes or did the laundry. Thus, after completing a year's service, the maid was dismissed. But Reb Bereleh generally helped those maids in one way or another. When one of his maidservants had to be married, he acted as close kinsman, helped with her dowry, and with other things important to the girl.

Tzirreleh, the current maidservant, happened to be in Pearl's good graces. That is why she remained in her job for several years. An orphan, and the daughter of a tenant farmer, in a remote village, she was sent to the city so that she would not be brought up among peasants. She was twelve years old when she arrived in Reb Bereleh's house. Pearl took pity on the orphan, and it never entered her mind to discharge the girl. She was a healthy youngster with rosy cheeks, energetic and industrious. Orphaned while still a child, she hardly remembered the faces of her parents. She was illiterate when she left the village, and was taught the rudiments of Jewishness in her new environment. The youngster matured into womanhood, and she regarded Reb Bereleh's house as her home, for she hardly knew anyone else.

2

Reb Bereleh spent very little time at home. He was always preoccupied with his affairs. He came home at night, his pockets bulging with pieces of paper, which he used to spread out on the table and then copied their contents into his account books. He was too oblivious to notice what was happening around him.

But there was one thing for which Reb Bereleh had time: moralizing. He preached morality to young and old. He ferreted out everyone's shortcomings and then exhorted them to keep to the straight and narrow. He even berated young men, but he did it jokingly. He rebuked especially girls and young men who went strolling across the wooden bridge into the forest on Sabbath afternoons. Reb Bereleh warned the parents that their sons and daughters were courting trouble, God forbid. Reb Bereleh moralized not rudely, but gently, and he did so to a cluster of townsmen in the marketplace but above all in the *shtibbel* of the Ger Hasidim. There he didn't spare anyone. Whatever was trumped up about the young generation digressing from the Mosaic Law, Reb Bereleh accepted as the intrinsic truth. He didn't tolerate any explanations or excuses about such matters. Thus, when he heard that a widow, residing in the suburbs, had rented a room to a man who was making the rounds of the villages, he became perturbed and set out to remonstrate with her.

"Mindel, the widow of Reb Aaron of blessed memory—I hope you don't mind my intrusion," he said to her, "but why do you permit a strange man to spend the night under your roof?"

Mindel blushed and was at a loss as to how to make Reb Bereleh understand that the tenant's rent was badly needed to supplement her scant income.

"Your excuses will not pass muster," he went on. "Whatever rent the man pays you, I'll reimburse you for it several times over. But a man staying with you under one roof—that cannot be tolerated."

When he realized that he had offended and possibly distressed the widow, Reb Bereleh became more conciliatory. "If it weren't for your late husband who prayed together with us in the Ger *shtibbel*, I wouldn't have thought of coming here to talk to you. We keep an eye on everybody. And don't think for one moment that I have discussed the matter with anyone, or that someone had authorized me to come here. I came here of my own free will, and I brought you this."

He handed her a wad of paper money and remarked, "Before Passover, God willing, I will reimburse you again for the rent."

3

On Sabbath mornings Reb Bereleh, wearing his or-

nate, flowery, Sabbath lounging robe, with the protrud-
ing ritual fringes, sat in the drawing room, poring over
Holy Writ. He looked serene, calm as a millpond. His
sparse, blond beard was well groomed. Reb Bereleh used
to drink a glass of tea before proceeding to the synagogue
for prayer, although the Hasidim of Ger shunned this
practice. The teapot was usually placed in the tile oven
on the eve of the Sabbath, where it was kept warm. And it
was a sort of tradition for the maidservant to give him a
glass of tea at that time, without his asking. The moment
he made himself comfortable in the drawing room,
Tzirreleh the maid lost no time in placing a glass of tea in
front of him.

This time, when Tzirreleh entered, he looked up from
the Talmudic folio and caught sight of her shabby dress,
but also of the firm breasts straining against the
shirtwaist . . . Her graceful body and her gorgeous
youthful face suddenly fascinated him so much that he
was tempted to embrace her and to kiss her. He gulped
down the tea, and when Tzirreleh asked if he cared for
another glass of tea, he was unable to utter a word, and
nodded approval.

On being served the second glass, Reb Bereleh seemed
to tingle with excitement that he could not shake off.
After she left, he tried to compose himself. Stroking his
beard, he tried once again to concentrate on the Talmud,
but the figure of Tzirreleh seemed to blur its words.

Following the *Havdalah** he stroked his beard, determined to shrug off all the disturbing thoughts and to get
back to reality. Several Jews were already waiting to
negotiate new deals and to finalize others. So he became
totally oblivious of Tzirreleh.

But the following morning when he picked up his

---

*Ceremony of ushering out the Sabbath, consisting of prayers and chants, and
of lighting a twisted candle.

prayer shawl and the phylacteries and hastened to the Ger *shtibbel* to pray with the first *minyan*, he seemed to hear her footsteps again and to taste the second glass of tea that she had served him.

Reb Bereleh draped the prayer shawl around his head and tried to turn a deaf ear to the evil thoughts. He realized that the *sitra akhra** had taken possession of him, that in order to extricate himself from it, he had to resort to superhuman self-control.

A quarrel that ensued in the *shtibbel* of the Ger Hasidim, one in which Reb Bereleh became embroiled, helped bolster his bewildered spirit. It concerned the hiring of a man who was to serve as both cantor and ritual slaughterer. The local community by and large favored an accomplished cantor, while the Ger congregation stressed the quality of piety and fear of God in the individual. Being the guiding star of the Ger congregation, Reb Bereleh became involved in the controversy that lingered on for months. He was a strong and persistent advocate of the Ger viewpoint. When the squabble abated, the Ger congregation had prevailed and Reb Bereleh was credited with the victory. And, indeed, who would defy Reb Bereleh? It was common knowledge that Reb Bereleh was adamant.

There was rejoicing and festivity in the Ger *shtibbel*. The quarrel had subsided, the opponents were reconciled, and everyone was glad that peace had come to the community at last. Personally, however, Reb Bereleh gained little. When the controversy ended and Tzirreleh served him a glass of tea, he was again beset by evil thoughts.

Reb Bereleh was still in his prime—in his early forties—but he looked older. During the early years of

*"The other side"—the company of Satan.

their marriage Reb Bereleh paid no attention to any other woman. But as time wore on his wife became completely preoccupied with business, turned scrawny, and her eyes grew shifty, as though she were counting petty cash. Reb Bereleh had second thoughts about his marriage. Every Sabbath, while drinking his tea, he looked at things in retrospect and concluded that he had been catapulted into a vicious circle, from which there seemed to be no escape.

On Sabbath mornings, in the past, when Reb Bereleh pored over Holy Writ, the folio was open in front of him. But lately he covered it with a large kerchief, and when someone passed the drawing room, he closed it. Reb Bereleh now took to browsing through volumes in which the exegetes discoursed on the lives of men and women. Then he turned to the commentators who interpreted the affairs of Bathsheba* and other women in biblical times.

Suddenly, he took an interest in a statute in the Mosaic Law that does not prohibit a man from availing himself of a maidservant as a concubine. The more he delved into this matter, the more he chastised himself, but he could not tear himself away from those folios. He recalled that long ago, he too had a dream about a woman. And it was not a mere dream. He had even seen her. It happened at the yeshivah, the Talmudical academy, that he attended. His teacher's daughter used to stroll out, holding a book. He caught sight of her through the window only a couple of times, but he was so fascinated by her that she appeared in his dreams. Even now, he visualized her slender figure and graceful legs, the two long braids cascading over her shoulders. But that could hardly be

---

*Bathsheba, wife of King David. In order to marry her, David engineered the death of her husband, Uriah the Hittite, for which he was reprimanded by the prophet Nathan.

mentioned at home. No one would believe that Bereleh the yeshivah student, had any contact with that *Litvak*, the Hebrew teacher, who was known to consume non-kosher food.

When Bereleh married, he was confronted by a new life. Little by little, he began to forget his teacher's daughter. At times he gazed at his wife, hoping to fathom some of his dream girl's traits in her—but to no avail. His wife Pearl's lackluster eyes, her bowed legs in cloth sandals, her clumsy gait, and her whistling voice, so unlike the dream girl's sonorous one, presented such a sharp contrast.

During the early years of his marriage, Reb Bereleh immersed himself in the study of a page of the Gemara, or a difficult passage in *Tosephot** or a *Midrash Rabbah*† in order to reconcile himself to the state of affairs. Things were even better during his visits to the Rabbi of Ger. In company with other Hasidim at the table of that spiritual leader, his anxieties would dissipate like fog in a bright sun.

Reb Bereleh's wife frowned upon his absenting himself during the holidays. But she prevailed in one instance. He stayed at home for Simchat Torah,* Rejoicing of the Law. So it became a tradition to prepare roast meat for the entire congregation of the Ger *shtibbel* for the festival. Following the divine service, the worshippers assembled in Reb Bereleh's house and without waiting for an invitation, pounced upon the long tables, snatching the food with their bare hands. They ate and drank standing up and their *l'chayyims*—their toasts "to life!"—could be heard outside. Reb Bereleh urged on his

---

*Heb. "addenda."
†A collection of aggadic midrashim.
‡Holiday marking the annual completion of the synagogue reading of the Pentateuch.

wife and Tzirreleh to replenish the dwindling food. And the latter brought in boiled tongues, meat loaves, and roasted ducks. After the lavish feast the tables were moved out of the way, and the assembled launched into a Hasidic dance, in which Reb Bereleh joined. He danced with consummate skill and with more exuberance and rapture than the others. While he was in that transport of delight, Tzirreleh, carrying a tray of goodies, happened to make her way through the Hasidic throng. Without thinking Reb Bereleh stretched out his hand and embraced her. It was done so adroitly that hardly anyone noticed it. Tzirreleh pretended to be oblivious of what transpired and proceeded with her task.

She returned to the kitchen, happy as a clam at high water. She recalled a scene from her childhood: when she played with Stashek. He was wont to tickle her now and then, and she would tingle with emotion. She did not want to compare the two instances. With Stashek, the scene occurred on the green meadow, whereas here it was amidst greasy platters filled with chewed bones and food scraps. She hurried to clean up, apprehensive lest Reb Bereleh's wife was tipped off about the incident. In that case she, Tzirreleh, was likely to become the scapegoat.

It was only after the throng departed, and she was by herself in the kitchen, that a sense of her loneliness dawned on Tzirreleh. Before this, she had felt as though she were among kinsmen and was considered to be one, that she shared in the affluence of the house to some extent. Now she sensed a void of sorts. There was no one in whom she could confide about her innermost emotions, nor anyone to gratify her need.

Reb Bereleh's wife then came into the kitchen, shouting, "Tzirreleh, stop wasting time! Get busy with the dishes!"

4

The night of Simchat Torah, Reb Bereleh fell asleep on the wide couch in the drawing room in his satin gabardine and high boots. His wife and their children were already sleeping soundly. The candles in the silver candlesticks were still flickering. Tzirreleh had been ordered to clean up, but since she was exhausted, she stretched out in the dark alcove adjacent to the kitchen.

Reb Bereleh slept fitfully, breathing heavily. It looked as though he was trying to rouse himself, but failed in his attempt. It was only when wagons passed by with their usual roar that Reb Bereleh jumped up and ran to the window, straining his ears to ascertain if someone was trying to break in or if there was a fire. The scene was soon quiet again. Only the barking of a dog rent the air, from time to time. Then he noticed that he was wearing the satin gabardine and remembered that it was the festival of Rejoicing of the Law. He entered the kitchen to wash his hands. The silence seemed strange to him. Could it be that his wife had not yet retired for the night? Returning to the kitchen, he noticed that the door to the alcove was open. He peered in and saw Tzirreleh, asleep on the bunk in her threadbare dress with the short white apron. Reb Bereleh hardly remembered ever seeing her in a new garment. One of her legs dangled from the bunk, while the other was completely exposed. His first impulse was to flee, but the liquor he had drunk had lowered his resistance, and he reclined on the edge of the bunk.

He could not take his eyes off Tzirreleh. He saw her breasts heave. He bent a little closer and was spellbound by the bewitching area between them. At first he wanted to say, "Go, get me a glass of tea," but he was deterred by the halo of her face. He was gazing at a virgin in full bloom for the first time. He sat there breathless, then he tried to get up, but seemed riveted to the bunk.

In her sleep, Tzirreleh thought the cat was licking her face, and that a flick of her hand would drive it off. One eyelid lifted a bit, then closed. She thought she had seen Reb Bereleh in the kitchen, but didn't open her eyes.

Reb Bereleh found himself on the horns of a dilemma: Had he really drunk so much that he aroused these desires in himself? But in the next moment someone seemed to whisper distinctly in his ears: "Man was created for love; and if he neglects it, he was created in vain . . ."

Reb Bereleh took these words definitely to be the oracular voice importuning him to derive pleasure from *Olam ha-zeh*, from this material world. He no longer visualized Tzirreleh as a child, but as the virgin that is extolled in the *Song of Songs*. The entire pleasure of *Alam ha-zeh* lay in front of him.

He stepped out to turn out the light in the drawing room. Then he slumped to the edge of the bunk with fear and trembling, lest she wake up raising a hue and cry. Tzirreleh now became conscious of hands groping on her body. She was about to shout, but at that moment she heard a gentle voice, pleading, "Tzirreleh, be silent."

Tzirreleh was frightened out of her wits, as she recognized the voice: His wife was likely to barge in.

"Reb Bereleh—*oi*, you?" the stupefied Tzirreleh whispered.

5

From the moment her pregnancy became discernible Reb Bereleh handed her money secretly. He was careful. When he went to the kitchen to wash his hands, he pronounced the appropriate benediction so she could hear him, and from behind the towel, he slipped her some paper money. She took the gratuity eagerly, and her spirits were raised.

"Save it. It will come in handy," he mumbled during the benediction.

Reb Bereleh is now fidgety and high-strung. At the drop of a hat he snaps and shouts at his wife. He no longer defers to her as he used to in the past. She pestered him about sending the wench away, as she grew more corpulent, and her garments had to be refitted, but he didn't let her. Reb Bereleh rebuked his wife, saying, "We must not be unjust to an orphan."

But his wife was losing her patience. Women, one after another, accosted her and demanded:

"Is your servant really pregnant?"

"Evidently she is in her fourth month."

"Any clue as to who it was?"

"Probably Gentile boys. She was warned not to meet the Gentile boys on the meadow."

It was the burning question in Reb Bereleh's house.

In the evening the women showed up and went into a huddle with his wife. Nekha, the cantor's wife, whispered piously, "Pearl, believe me, the best way out is for you to take her away to a home for foundlings in Warsaw, where servants are accommodated until after their confinement. Velveleh, the coachman, knows all about these things."

Now and then, Tzirreleh overheard some of the whispers, but she made light of it. She was occupied with her own problem. As the life stirred inside her, Reb Bereleh was more appealing to her. She yearned to take hold of his hand and to place it on her belly, where she felt the new life stirring. She arose at the crack of dawn, before he left for the synagogue to pray with the first *minyan,* though he avoided the kitchen. This caused her such anguish that she dropped things: then a glass of hot milk that she fetched for Reb Bereleh's wife.

Pearl noticed that her husband was in a bad mood, and she attributed this to the wanton wench's hobnobbing with Gentile boys, and the resultant disgrace to the household. She was not eager to have Velveleh, the coachman, come to the house, so she asked him to arrange the transportation of Tzirreleh to Warsaw and paid the fare in advance. Then she hurried home and said to her husband, "Tomorrow morning, I'm sending away the wench."

The following morning Pearl arose when it was still dark. Reb Bereleh, too, got dressed. He wanted to see her off. He was about to present her with something. He paced to and fro, holding a towel, waiting for Tzirreleh to get up.

Pearl got into the kitchen and shouted, "Tzirreleh, get up!"

The alcove was quiet.

"Did you ever see such a wench? You holler, and she pretends not to hear." Pearl shouted even louder.

Then she opened the door to the alcove to find that Tzirreleh had left. The pillows and the featherbed that she had brought from her village were on the wooden bunk. Pearl looked in the other rooms and in the courtyard. Then she ran into the drawing room, screaming, "She is gone!"

PSALMS

No one knew him in the little community. Only a few of the residents had ever seen him with a sack on his back, heading for the village in the morning.

He kept to himself, speaking to no one. Occasionally, when he encountered another Jew he mumbled "Good morning," and went on his way.

Maybe he was ashamed of himself because of his shabby attire. He wore patched hand-me-downs, and the hem of his long jacket was held together by a hemp rope. Maybe he was a little crazy.

He might have gone through life like that, without anyone paying the least attention to him, if it hadn't been for the disastrous epidemic that did not spare a single Jewish home.

Reb Abbala, the local rabbi, tried all sorts of rituals and prayers to stamp out the plague. He led collective recitations of the Psalms for days on end, in front of the open Holy Ark. He lit candles, visited ancestral graves and intoned special prayers. But it was of no avail. The only conclusion anyone could draw was that the community was guilty of some inexpiable sin.

Reb Abbala racked his brain to find the culprits who might have dealt with heathens and with drunks. He thought about every widow and spinster in town. But he didn't have the heart to denounce anyone or to lodge a complaint against any specific household, as the source of evil. Meanwhile, the pestilence continued to take a horrendous toll.

Before the outbreak of the epidemic, the Jewish dead were buried in the cemetery of a neighboring town, because no such facilities were available to the community. All the vacant fields surrounding the town belonged to the local priest, a wicked man, who was adamant in his refusal to sell a tract of land to the Jews for this purpose. But when the pestilence struck, the neighboring town prohibited further burials, fearing that the epidemic would spread to them. At that time, the priest was on a pilgrimage to Rome. A delegation of Jews then purchased a sandy tract from the administrator. However, the latter stipulated that if the priest, upon his return, disallowed the transfer of property, then the initial payment would be forfeited and the tract had to be cleared.

By the time the priest returned, the tract was dotted with quite a few graves. He ordered the overseer to annul the contract and the dead exhumed.

Reb Abbala sent emissaries with gifts to the priest. He almost decreed that the women present the priest with some of their jewelry. But the wicked man swore at them like a soldier and relentlessly kept to his stand.

When the emissaries had failed, Reb Abbala visited the priest in person, saying, "I came to you because I am in the situation of our Father Abraham who had to plead with the children of Heth for the possession of a burying place."

The priest wasn't polite enough to ask the rabbi in, but listened to him on the threshold and then interrupted him rudely. "You are not Father Abraham and I am not of the children of Heth. I don't want to have any Jewish bones in my field."

"But just look at what's going on in town," Reb Abbala pleaded, holding back his tears.

"Unless you order the dead exhumed right now, I will do it myself and throw them to the dogs!" the priest snapped.

Reb Abbala was about to implore him again, but the priest unceremoniously shut the door in his face.

On his way home the downhearted rabbi wept bitterly, for he was well aware that the priest could carry out his threat. "What's to be done? What's to be done?" he kept muttering to himself.

The woebegone spiritual leader was groping ahead, tapping his cane on the road at a loss about how to help his fellow Jews in their new predicament.

He was suddenly stopped by a young man in tatters with a sack on his back. "Rabbi, why are you crying?"

Reb Abbala raised his tear-stained eyes and looked at the shabbily dressed stranger. He thought it a waste of time to try to explain the situation to someone who was not likely to be of any help.

"Rabbi, you must tell me!" the stranger persisted.

Reb Abbala sensed that he couldn't get rid of this fellow so easily, and in his desperation he wanted to unburden himself. And so he told the young man about the priest's threat to exhume the dead and fling them to the dogs.

The young man was quiet at first, even simple-minded, but now he was entirely transformed. His eyes blazed, he threw off the sack and drew closer to the rabbi. "Rabbi, stop crying and listen to what I tell you."

The rabbi pulled himself together and the young man resumed. "May he be consumed by fire! Let the wicked man croak! I'll teach him a lesson! He'll be struck by lightning this very day!"

Although Reb Abbala opined that the priest deserved such punishment, he could not tolerate vehement curses on the part of this coarse fellow. Looking askance at him, he hurried away.

Reb Abbala did not lose sight of his only weapon—Psalms. Once again he summoned a group of Jews and they intoned the Psalms in front of the Holy Ark, weeping fervently. Some even tore their garments as a sign of mourning, hoping to ward off the plague.

It was a bright sunny day with a crystal blue sky—one of the finest summer days. But the hearts of the Psalm narrators were gloomy, and their laments stirred the soul.

That afternoon, the sky suddenly became overcast. Lightning struck and it thundered so ferociously that the windows rattled. A cloudburst inundated the streets. It seemed as though heaven and earth joined the Psalm narrators in mourning.

The worshippers were alarmed. They had a premonition that Satan was getting the upper hand. But Reb Abbala, precisely because of the storm, did not authorize an intermission in the reading of the Psalms. He maintained that during the moments of lightning, the gates of heaven are open and through pleading one can obtain whatever his heart desires.

After the storm had subsided, a Jew rushed in, and shouted out of breath, "The priest has just been struck by lightning."

Reb Abbala sat there, overwhelmed. He felt intuitively that the curse of the stranger with the sack on his back had come true. He was distressed because he had behaved disrespectful to the *nistor*—a saint who hides his true identity. How can you account for the fact that such a young man in shabby garb, has a voice in heaven? He only uttered something, and his wish was granted!

"He'll be struck by lightning this very day!" The young man's vehement curse still echoed in the rabbi's ears. Why, thought the rabbi, the young man didn't even put off. He didn't wait for an opportune moment. He had said *today*. It is obvious that the event was not something ordinary. Indeed, throughout the day there was not a cloud in the sky, then, suddenly, there was a thunderstorm that uprooted trees. And thunder and lightning. There were shepherds in the fields, horses in the streets, tall poplar trees, and drenched peasants ran home from the fields. But no one else was hurt, only that wicked man who made me cry. The young man, seeing me cry, had pronounced a curse on the priest's head. He wanted to set my mind at ease.

The people gathered in the House of Study were happy about the doom of the wicked priest. But when they looked at the rabbi, they found him to be pale and trembling. He was sitting in his wide pew, at the eastern wall, facing the congregation. With one hand he covered his eyes, which saw the young man with the sack on his back. Who was the mysterious person he had talked to? He was at his wits' end. Could it be that he would never see the young man again? He asked if anyone knew about the stranger, a young man with a sack on his back.

No one remembered such a person. Then it dawned on someone that the rabbi was probably referring to the fellow who made the rounds of the villages. This young man wandered through villages during the weekdays, and returned only for the Sabbath—but had never come to the House of Study.

Listening to this account the congregants were astonished. They soon concluded that there was more to these events than met the eye. There was something unusual about it. However, no one dared to press the rabbi for an explanation. They hoped to get to the bottom of the incident, somehow.

Knitting his brow, the rabbi asked, "Does anyone know his name?"

And when no one answered him, the rabbi continued,

"How do you account for the fact that no one can identify the young man who has been around here? And why don't I know him?"

"In that case, rabbi, we will bring him here, to the House of Study."

That is what Reb Abbala wanted. But he hastened to add, "Not to the House of Study, but to my house."

The congregants were even more astonished at this. The rabbi did not usually invite such people to his house.

The moment the young man opened the door, Reb Abbala stepped forward to welcome him. Then he drew the visitor to the alcove and tried to engage him in a discussion of profound issues. He was particularly interested in learning the identity of the young man. But the young man did not understand the complicated Hebrew words that the rabbi used. Finally he blurted out, "Rabbi, talk to me in simple Yiddish."

Reb Abbala now began to have second thoughts about his visitor, and turned the conversation to more prosaic matters.

"What's your name?"

"Hershel"

"How do you earn your livelihood?"

"With the grace of God, rabbi."

Reb Abbala now regretted his having second thoughts about the young man. For there did indeed seem to be something otherworldly about him. The more he camouflages, thought the rabbi, the more conceivable his eminence.

When Hershel sighed, Reb Abbala said, "Hershel, what do you need?" thus hoping to draw him out.

But Hershel answered simply, "A bride, with God's grace, a wife, rabbi."

Scrutinizing his visitor, the rabbi remarked, "What made you think of this in the midst of the epidemic?"

"Because—because I am annoyed by evil thoughts, and I must resist them as one resists mad dogs. Those thoughts cut into my time for divine service."

Reb Abbala was at an impasse. But then he beamed as though a vision had come from Divine Providence. "So that's it!" he exclaimed. "Evil thoughts in a young man's mind are likely to bring about an epidemic."

Reb Abbala was considerably relieved. He thought the key to warding off the epidemic had been handed to him. Furthermore, the match for the young man seemed to have been signaled to him directly from heaven: Khinka, the orphaned girl who worked as a maid. She was beautiful and pious, the people said, but she had no luck. She was always occupied, and was rarely seen in public. Once in a while she visited the rabbi to inquire about a judicial matter. And on the Sabbath, so the account runs, she stayed indoors the whole day, learning how to pray from her mistress. The question of marrying the orphan had come up time and again, but no bridegroom was available. All these thoughts now flashed through the rabbi's mind.

"Hershel!" Reb Abbala exclaimed. "Just as you put an end to the life of a wicked priest, so you shall put an end to the epidemic! Khinka, a beautiful, kosher daughter will be your bride. And I insist that the marriage ceremony should take place in the cemetery."

Hershel squirmed and fell silent.

"Why don't you answer?" the rabbi pressed him.

"Rabbi, you are demanding too much from me," Hershel blurted out.

"I think I've got him now," thought the rabbi.

"Rabbi, I would like to ask you something," the young man said after some hesitation.

"By all means."

"Is it justified to engage a beautiful Jewish girl to a

poor homeless person, whose identity no one knows?"
Hershel pursued.

That took the rabbi's breath away. But he realized that
unless he mastered the situation, the epidemic would
continue.

"I say it is justifiable and just. You are allowed to
marry Khinka, and she will consent," the rabbi answered.

"Is this a verdict, a legal decision, rabbi?"

"Yes, Hershel. It is a verdict which cannot be ap-
pealed."

"In that case, rabbi, I want you to issue another verdict
right after the marriage ceremony."

"Yes?"

"That the epidemic in the city shall come to an end."

That same day the rabbi called the dignitaries of the
community together, to inform them of his meeting with
Hershel. The townspeople took up a collection and
rented a shack for the prospective newlyweds. In addition they purchased two wooden pails and a yoke.

The whole community turned out to attend the marriage which took place in the cemetery. The epidemic
gradually subsided.

The townspeople had all but forgotten about the
epidemic though Hershel's curse on the wicked was still
talked about.

Hershel became the local water carrier. When he
delivered water to a home, it was as though he also
delivered luck. The people were delighted to give him a few
groshens—and he brought all the money to his wife,
begrudging himself even a single coin.

Khinka, his wife, was good-natured and endowed with
great beauty. The shack, with its earthen floor was poorly
furnished, and there were no cupboards. No photographs
of Talmudical sages adorned the interior, nor were there

any copper pans in the kitchen. But the brass candlesticks shone like pure gold and the *hallah* tablecloth was a
dazzling white.

She moved around the shanty like a gentle dove, and
welcomed her husband with affection and esteem. On
entering his home, Hershel placed the pails and the yoke
in a corner near the door. Then he washed up and
pronounced a benediction and finally sat down to his
meager meal.

Hershel was finished with his deliveries of water by
noon, since few households could afford such luxury. The
rest of the day, Hershel usually spent with Reb Abbala.
The rabbi became his friend and appointed him assis-
tant sexton. His duties were to sweep and illuminate the
House of Study and to attend to related chores.

Hershel was fond of extensive prayer. Indeed, his chant
to the Almighty was enigmatic and differed from the
traditional way. Some regarded him as an ignoramus
who prayed the wrong way because he did not know the
text of the *Siddur,* as was the case of the unenlightened.
Others, including Reb Abbala, deemed his way of prayer
to be that of a mysterious *Tzaddik,* or sage. Hershel
preferred to pray alone and to do so at his leisure,
uttering each word distinctly. But all the same he found
it grueling to follow the text of the *Siddur.* Some passages
he intoned in Yiddish, by heart. He prayed with great
fervor, but it was the Psalms he savored the most. When
he intoned Psalms in his mellifluous sing-song, it was as
though King David played on his lyre.

Though he devoted considerable time to the divine
service, he could not find peace of mind.

"A man's service to the Lord is not enough. He has to
get others to do the same," Hershel once said to his wife.
The latter agreed.

Thereafter he arose at the crack of dawn, kissed the

mezuzah * and made the rounds of the town, rousing the people to recite the Psalms. His melodious voice echoed everywhere, through the cracks in the shutters, penetrated the hearts of the sleeping Jews. Even little children recognized the sing-song.

Hershel's rallying cry, "Fellow Jews, arise to recite the Psalms," carried an exhilarating note. Some maintained that his voice reached the gates of heaven.

Reb Shloima Aiger, the eminent scholar, happened to be in town for the Sabbath. On hearing Hershel's rallying cry, "Fellow Jews, arise to recite the Psalms," he felt that the melodious voice kindled within him special fervor for the divine service. He had been aroused to recite Psalms on many occasions, but he had never heard a voice that inbued him with such devotion. He thought that an ordinary sexton was not likely to be endowed with such a voice, a voice that can open all the seven heavens. He was consumed with curiosity about Hershel and arranged for the latter to serve him.

Reb Shloima Aiger followed Hershel's trail everywhere, but found nothing bizarre about him. But he still thought that Hershel was no ordinary human being, and he made several attempts to engage him in a profound discussion. Hershel invariably was able to sidetrack such conversation. At times the sage concluded that Hershel was a common man, a son of the soil. At other times, he felt that Hershel was close-mouthed and transcendental, reluctant to reveal his identity. He could not tell.

"Rabbi, is one permitted to address God in plain Yiddish?" Hershel once asked the sage.

Reb Shloima Aiger looked at him good-naturedly and remarked, "One can address God even without words,

---

*Small tube containing a piece of parchment on which are inscribed verses from Deuteronomy 6:4-9 and 11:13-21, attached to the doorpost of observant Jews.

because the language that God understands is the one that issues from a person's heart. The more saintliness a person possesses when he approaches his conception of God, the more elegant the language, because He is omniscient."

Hershel's eyes now shined like stars.

One day Reb Shloima Aiger remarked, "Hershel, sing something."

"God forbid!"

"Why?"

"I can't sing."

"Why do you call the people to recite the Psalms with such a beautiful voice then?"

"That's something different, that's in the service of the Lord."

After the brief dialogue, Reb Shloima Aiger realized his mistake. Throughout his life he had avoided being served by a Talmudic scholar. Now he was served by a "Lamed Vovnik."* For a moment he tried to disavow the thought. He could have been mistaken, such things do happen. But no, his sharp eye didn't deceive him. Hershel could very well have been a holy man who preferred to live in hiding. Then he must not be held back.

The day after his talk with Hershel, the elders of the community visited the sage to discuss an important matter with him. Before they left, one of them asked if the sage was pleased with his quarters.

"Yes, indeed, everything is fine," the sage replied. "But isn't there someone else in your community who can serve me?"

"How's that? What about Hershel?"

"Everything is all right," Reb Shloima Aiger said, "but a man of great means is serving me. There are many

*One of 36 righteous men on whom the continued existence of the world depends.

affluent men in Warsaw but this affluent man who serves me is most uncommon. He is a firebrand, who is inspired to divine service and who is endowed with a good Jewish heart, loving kindness and the fervor of *tzaddikim.* Such rich men are indeed rare! Isn't there some poor man in your community who can serve me?"

The elders exchanged glances in disbelief.

"Who does the sage mean?" one of them asked.

"Who?" another interposed. "Don't you understand that he means Hershel?"

"None other than Hershel?"

"Well, what do you know? Who would have thought?"

PRIDE AND JOY

Bunim's *heder*, the traditional religious school, was located on the busiest street in town. In order to get to the marketplace you had to go down that thoroughfare, which was always in tumult—especially on a fair day when the neighing of horses, the bleating of sheep, the lowing of cattle, merged with the shouts of the traders. The melodious sing-song of the pupils studying the Torah in Bunim's *heder* echoed through the marketplace. At times it seemed as though people held their breaths to hear the children's melodious voices. When Jewish pedestrians heard the Torah chant of the youngsters, they slowed down. The intonation of the biblical text ushered them into another world. That was particularly true of those whose children attended Bunim's *heder*. They were imbued with a conceit that they too had a share in the world to come.

Bunim was selective in the enrollment of pupils to his *heder*. He was as painstaking as in the selection of rare gems. Children of the affluent were given no preference. Money was not the decisive factor, God forbid. He was primarily interested in talented youngsters. And when one of the pupils grasped some abstruse passage in Holy Writ, he was enraptured. For that pupil he spared no efforts, treating him as he would his own child. Bunim believed that many of his pupils would grow up to be erudite Talmudists. He taught them the Gemara and the Tosaphot—they were already well versed in the Pentateuch and Rashi—the initial steps set them off in the right direction.

Some of the parents were prompt in paying the tuition, but many were unable to meet their obligations. Bunim was not concerned. He treated all: the son of the affluent dignitary and the son of the struggling peddler who made the rounds of the villages the same. Only in his pinching did he discriminate, but not, God forbid, according to worldly status. When a pupil was perceptive and understood the lesson in the Talmud he got a slight pinch on the cheek. One who failed to comprehend the lesson got a painful pinch. And Bunim kept after the youngster until he mastered the moot point.

Bunim was in seventh heaven when his pupils were engrossed in their study and their Gemara sing-song reverberated beyond the confines of the *heder.* Hinda Leah, Bunim's wife, rejoiced in the diligent study of the pupils, and took care of them as though they were her own children. She broiled potatoes, and on Hanukah* she served them pancakes. In the winter, when they left school in the evening, she helped light their tiny lanterns, buttoned their coats, tied scarfs around their necks, and ushered them out with loving care.

It is natural to love children, even someone else's. There is nothing unusual about that, particularly for a Jewish mother. But it was uncommon in the case of Hinda Leah, because none of her own children had lived—may you be spared such a fate. She gave birth to several children, but in each instance some sinister fate seemed to pluck them out of the cradle. With her affection for other people's children she may have been trying to get the fateful decree revoked. It preyed on her mind. She secluded herself for days on end, weeping, sometimes quietly and sometimes loudly. Her behavior interfered with the pupils' instruction, and then Bunim

---

*The eight-day celebration commemorating the victory of Judah Maccabee over Antiochus Epiphanes.

was about to upbraid her, but on catching sight of her tearful eyes, he held his tongue. Because of all her crying, her eyelashes were stripped, and her eyes appeared blind. During her wailing she complained about certain grievances, including the fact that no one would recite the mourner's *kaddish* for her.

Bunim did not lose his temper, was not bitter, did not fret and fume against the Lord. He accepted all blows submissively. He assumed they were decreed by the Almighty. Occasionally, however, he became disheartened. This happened when he took stock of his life, trying to unearth some sin that would justify the harshness of his fate. But he found not a hint of transgression. At such time, he was distressed, the pupils looked at their teacher pacing to and fro, his hairy chest exposed, and the ritual fringes flowing. He stopped near his wife, his beard trembling, to shriek, "I will not keep quiet! I will not rest! I will visit one *tzaddik* after another, until we're granted salvation!"

Hinda Leah burst into tears and sighed with relief. She knew that her redemption lay in a *tzaddik*'s blessing.

But when Bunim visited the *tzaddik* and spoke about his trials and tribulations, about his children dying in their infancy and about his wife's grief, the spiritual leader hedged and sidestepped the subject. His host asked irrelevant questions about how many pupils Bunim had in the *heder*, and whether they were God-fearing, but he studiously ignored the questions in the note handed to him. Then it dawned on Bunim that the "gates were closed." After this, he did not visit the sages anymore.

When he could no longer endure his wife's anguish, which had aged her prematurely, he resolved to spare no effort. He set out at dawn to visit the *tzaddik;* and this time he intended not to return empty-handed. He insisted on a promise from his host.

His task was by no means easy. "Rabbi, please give me your blessing!"

When Bunim became aware that the sage was hesitating again about giving him the coveted blessing, he broke out in a sweat, and blurted out, "Rabbi, I will do anything as long as a son survives me! I'm not leaving without your blessing!"

Only then did the spiritual leader respond, "Well, Bunim, since you insist that your son should have a long life, I bestow my blessing upon you!"

The sage placed both his hands on Bunim's head and slowly intoned "May it be the Will—that your son, Yudel still in his cradle, should have a long life!"

Removing his hands from the head of his guest, the spiritual leader said, "Remember, Bunim, you said, you'll do anything."

Bunim was relieved. He hurried home to inform his wife of the good news that their son would have a long life.

Hinda Leah had the most difficult childbirth with Yudel. The infant was bigger than the children born before him. He came into the world with a loud cry uncommon for an infant. He tossed and turned in the cradle, so that he almost upset it. And when he was hungry, he screamed to high heaven. He became really mischievous when he was able to walk. He smashed and demolished everything he came into contact with. He even turned over the water barrel.

His parents trembled with fear for the newborn. They dressed him in white, and on the slightest excuse they conjured up an evil eye. At the approach of some elderly peasant, who was reputed to be a witch, they rushed the infant into the house.

Yudel matured into a sturdy lad. Sometimes he ran outside chasing the ponies and rode the goats. He was the apple of their eye.

Finally Bunim had the satisfaction of seating his son beside the other pupils in front of an open prayer book, with the pointer on the page. It didn't take Bunim long to figure out that it would be a Herculean task to teach his son the rudiments of Hebrew lore. But he took comfort in the fact that his son would grow into a good householder. When Yudel was still quite young, he helped his mother sweep the floor, set benches in order, put out the garbage, place wet firewood to dry under the tile oven. Later on, he fetched water that he pumped himself, he chopped wood, and on occasion, when his mother bought a sack of potatoes and the peasant was reluctant to deliver it, little Yudel hauled it home. Bunim then rebuked his wife, remarking that such chores could bring on curvature of the spine. But Yudel adjusted his cap jauntily, laughed at the whole thing, and whistled in his father's face.

Yudel grew by leaps and bounds, maturing into a stalwart lad. His mother was apprehensive about the evil eye, and did not talk about how he escaped all the children's ailments. The boy turned out to be unruly and recalcitrant. Being a diligent pupil in the *heder* was out of the question. Now and then, Bunim scolded him, but to no avail. He taught the youngster how to pray, but his other efforts were in vain. Yudel was out of the house most of the time. He picked apples in someone's orchard, or threw stones at someone's pigeons, and when an irate neighbor scolded him, he retaliated by breaking the neighbor's windows at night. Thus, people were afraid of him.

The Gentile neighbors, however, thought well of him. They praised Hinda Leah for having such a sturdy son who would make a good soldier and horseman, and some of their impudent women even confided that their daughters were infatuated with him.

So the parents doted on Yudel during his childhood and Bunim saw himself in the boy, his broad-shouldered, athletic build, as well as Hinda Leah's sparkling dark eyes. But when his muscular arms developed Bunim recalled the passage, "The hands are the hands of Esau."

Brooding about the situation, Bunim was alarmed by the thought that his beloved son was growing up to be unruly. And he recalled the rabbi's hesitation in giving him the coveted blessing. Who can fathom the thoughts of the *tzaddikim*, who envision things through divine inspiration, he reasoned. Bunim's *heder* was teeming with lovely, graceful youngsters. But someone was missing, his son. At every sound, each time the door opened, he looked around anxiously, hoping that his son was coming home.

But Yudel seldom came home. In time, he became more unruly, more of an incorrigible rascal. He hobnobbed with the scum of the earth. It was rumored that he frequented Gentile taverns. He came home late at night, and sometimes he didn't come home at all. His mother pleaded with him to at least put on the phylacteries during the morning prayers, but it was useless.

On a fair day some children did not attend *heder*. The merchants informed Bunim that their children had to help out with minor chores and to keep an eye on peasants who were tempted to make off with some of the merchandise. The youngsters relished a fair day. From time to time they sneaked out from the shops to roam through the marketplace. They thrilled to watch Yudel whip up the ponies. Bunim wondered why Yudel came home agitated and bruised, his feet grimy, and his pants torn on fair days. The pupils chuckled as they recounted how Yudel alternately goaded some horses and rode others as they were tried out by would-be buyers. He would take charge of a young bucking bronco to see if it was recalcitrant and would rear on its haunches. Bunim questioned his pupils when the boy was away. Listening to their tales, Bunim became so upset that his hair almost stood at end. They told him how Hershel Ribak, the horse trader, haggled, driving a hard bargain, slapping one another's hands, until they were red, and when a sale was consummated, all of them, including Yudel, adjourned to the saloon. They did not know what went on in the saloon, because they were barred from it. Thus Yudel became a drunk and a lowlife. When outlaws followed a peasant who had just sold a horse and had a full purse, Yudel acted as the lookout.

Bunim was so eloquent that he could influence many people, but not his son. The more he tried to persuade him, the more his efforts boomeranged. The father alternated between being rational and austere, and being lenient and pleading. He described Gehenna (Hell), where the wicked were boiled in casks of seething pitch, and where they rolled down slopes of shattered glass naked on their way to the gates of hell. Or coming out, tarred with pitch, they carry heavy sacks filled with sins, the more sins, the heavier their sack. The wicked must struggle under such burdens for eternity.

Listening to his chastising words, Hinda Leah burst into tears and wailed, "Yudel, why do you torture me so? Why do I deserve such a fate? Oh, woe is me!"

But the more his father argued and the more his mother wailed, the more arrogant and spiteful their son became. Bunim clung to a shred of consolation: that the tales told about his son were made-up, or exaggerated.

But once Bunim chanced to witness something that really upset him. He saw his son smoking publicly on the Sabbath. If a hole had opened in the earth in front of him, he would have sunk into it. He tore at his hair. To desecrate the holy Sabbath! Why, the world was coming to an end! Yudel continued in his own ways, committing even more abominable sins, and humiliating his parents before God and man. His parents grew prematurely gray and old.

For the life of him, Bunim could not understand where Yudel got the money to buy a pair of new boots with lacquered tops. He was even more chagrined at the thought that Yudel wore his short coat on the Sabbath, just as on a weekday. On Sunday, or on a Gentile holiday, he spruced up in the officer's boots, the wide trousers, and the tight-fitting jacket that buttoned all the way up. He put on leather gloves and slipped his knife into the pocket of his trousers. Bunim was astounded to see this. The lad was handsome and strong with curly hair, and sprouted a moustache. He had a habit of looking into his mother's mirror before leaving.

Yudel came to be known for his physical prowess. A blow of his right hand could send a person reeling. The peasants didn't believe that he was Jewish. They did not know that a Jew, too, can take care of himself. On the occasions when Yudel came to the *heder*, the pupils looked at the heroic lad with awe and admiration. But his parents saw a *goy* and another Esau in him.

Bunim's friends tried to console the unhappy man and his wife by saying that their son had a Jewish heart. It was rumored that when Yudel saw a Jewish porter struggling under a heavy load, he relieved him of it, and delivered it to its destination. Once he knocked out a peasant who tried to rob and beat a Jew. He protected Jews who were threatened. When a gang of Gentile hoodlums dragged Nakhtcha, the orphan, under the bridge, Yudel risked his life to rescue her. But these stories about their son were hardly a consolation for the parents. They would rather have seen him pale and scrawny, attending the *heder*, growing up a prodigy.

Little by little, Bunim's *heder* changed. There was little fervor and diligence left in his teaching. He moped about, brooding over the rabbi's words. Why did he insist? Bunim's appearance and behavior reflected his inner turmoil. Some townsmen, aware of the situation, enrolled their children in another *heder*. Bunim was reconciled to this turn of events. He did not plead with the disgruntled parents to change their minds. He was absorbed by the fact that his son, who was reared in the merit of the rabbi's blessing, had matured into a heathen, stranger.

One hot summer day, when the sun burned and the shingle roofs were like a tinder box, a house caught fire. The flames quickly spread to the street where the House of Study was. The roaring fire engulfed one residence after another. The heat was suffocating. Some hard-pressed residents tossed bedding out of the windows; others left everything to the mercy of God. Mothers fled the scene, hugging their infants. The fire brigade arrived with barrels of water, but by that time the conflagration was out of control. The raging flames consumed everything in their path. Before long the House of Study itself was blazing.

"Save the holy scrolls of the Torah!" alarmed Jews screamed.

While others in the panic-stricken throng were afraid to risk their lives, Yudel dashed into the burning synagogue, groping his way through the clouds of dense smoke and the fire. He succeeded in his mission. Within a few minutes he emerged, clutching the holy scrolls of the Torah, his blackened face and hands scorched, flames licking his garments. Still gripping the scrolls, he started to dance, then he collapsed and fainted.

The rabbi and the elders of the community, who witnessed the heroic feat, pronounced a benediction and eulogized the Lord for the miracle, and blessed the young hero for his achievements.

The semi-conscious Yudel was oblivious to the turmoil around him. When he was revived in the hospital, he caught sight of his parents, the rabbi, and the local dignitaries. The rabbi asked Yudel to repeat after him the *Gomel* benediction, which is recited for someone who risked his life for *Kiddush ha-Shem*, for the Sanctification of the Name. The rabbi praised the Lord of the Universe for His grace.

Yudel came to be known as a hero and savior, and instead of being condemned and cursed, he was now showered with blessings.

As an ardent Hasid and a God-fearing man, Bunim saw the hand of God and the blessing of the old spiritual leader in the miracle. Shortly after this he visited the old rabbi, and the two talked for a long time. Bunim was reluctant to reveal the subject they discussed. All he would say was that when he departed the old rabbi said, "Bunim, go home in health and in peace, and resume your teaching of the Torah to the children."

And when Bunim paused in the doorway, with a quizzical look on his face, the rabbi added, "Were it not for the rescue of the Torah, Yudel would still be a nobody, as you know. And the fact that he mingled with the heathens, and imitated their prowess, was merely in order to prepare him for the coming performance of the *Kiddush ha-Shem*. And because you behaved the way you did until the miracle happened, you and your wife have earned the rewards of this world and the world to come."

Bunim returned home exhilarated and strengthened. He regained his courage and yearned to teach. And once again he indulged in the study of the Torah with his pupils.

TZALKA THE MATCHMAKER

Tzalka the matchmaker looked like a typical matchmaker—short, humble, talkative, with a sparse yellow goatee. His broadcloth cap with the small visor and narrow top, was always shoved back on his head, so that his huge, scholarly forehead was more visible. Maybe his cap was black at one time, but the sun had faded it so that it was now colorless. In the summer, he walked leaning on his cane, which had a white bone handle and a steel ferrule tip. It struck the sidewalk with a familiar click, so that anyone could tell when Tzalka was approaching. When he was in a good mood, he carried the cane mischievously on his shoulder. In the winter, the cane was replaced by a wide umbrella which he carried regardless of the weather. In the summer, he wore a torn alpaca robe; and in the winter, a topcoat with a sheepskin collar. Throughout the year, he wore the same cowhide boots which had long been in need of new vamps and heels but were beyond his means. He was poverty-stricken all his life, yet he never complained. He was always in a good mood, and humming a tune.

Tzalka was friendly with both the affluent and the poor. He knew how to communicate with all sorts of characters. At Jewish weddings, he was in his element, like a member of the family, because in most instances he was the matchmaker. That is why he regarded his calling not as something casual, but as an important mission— as was the case, for instance, with the religious leaders who rendered noteworthy service to the community. And what was more important than to see that Jewish daughters did not remain spinsters? God forbid. Without

Tzalka, the town would indeed be in a sorry state, he used to say. First God, then Tzalka. He used to say this at the drop of a hat. Particularly when he had a few drinks, he went into the soliloquy:

"What would have happened with blind Leah's daughter, eh! If I hadn't stepped in, she would have stayed an old maid. Who else thought to persuade Joel the teamster to marry her, down-and-out, without any dowry at all? But with Tzalka nothing is impossible. When Tzalka decides to arrange a match, he always succeeds and he knows that Providence lends a hand. Or take for instance the ironmonger's high and mighty daughter, who looked down her nose at everybody—assuming that a nobleman would arrive in a coach-and-four to court her. But as soon as the first gray streak appeared in her hair, her father began to badger me. And who else but Tzalka was instrumental in getting her a bridegroom? True, he is only a musician—and not so young at that—nor a big shot as she fancied, but when he plays the violin, the melody can melt your heart."

Nothing distressed Tzalka more than when someone said, "Watchmaker and matchmaker are the humblest professions—if they can at all be referred to as such." Tzalka flushed as though he had had a third drink, and his cap trembled. His ego was hurt, he was like a rabbi who is offended if he is told that he is incompetent to judge moot points in the *Halachah*. He was ready to lash out at such critics. Knowing his sensitivity, jolly Yeshivah students used to chide him:

"Well, Reb Tzalka, did you succeed in making a match today?"

Some bold young men who had already shortened their sidelocks and discarded the traditional long robes loved to tease him and address him a bit more arrogantly:

"Reb Tzalka, you intrude into God's domain . . . Once

someone asked 'What does the Lord do?' And he was answered, 'He makes matches.' But don't you depend on Him? And, as a matter of fact, you earn your livelihood that way.''

Tzalka was hurt to the core by such challenges. But he persisted in his calling, which one may say he cherished. For hours on end he sat browsing through his thick notebook. Its black covers had deteriorated long ago. Young men were listed in one section of the notebook, girls in another; and next to each name was a memorandum that only he could decipher. He divided the girls into three categories. He could identify a type by glancing at the memorandum. Thus, the letters "FD" signified "fat dowry." The letter "D" by itself meant "ordinary dowry." It was worse, however, when the letters "DPBND" accompanied a given name, for it meant "Dowry promised but not delivered."

However, such a memorandum was inadequate. Nor was he duty-bound to remember other specifics. So he added supplementary marks. Thus, the letter "B" stood for "Beautiful," "RS" stood for "Rachel's sister," that is, the bride had the muddy eyes of the biblical Leah. And when a girl was getting along in years, he jotted down the word "twice."

Tzalka guarded his notebook with the shoddy covers like the apple of his eye. At night he placed it under his pillow. He knew that all his possessions were in the notebook. On Hanukah he reviewed his notebook, writing in new names and deleting old ones. It continued to be his source of livelihood.

When a young man and his girlfriend caught his attention, he was determined to steer them to holy wedlock. But when his task proved formidable, as when the young man and his friend preferred to stay single—who knows, maybe they were carrying on in the forest, as is customary with contemporary youth—or when the girl

walked out on her suitor—Tzalka was dismayed. It was
not so much the forfeiture of the matchmaker's fee that
bothered him as the fact that he had failed in his mission.
He stood for hours, draped in his prayer shawl and phylacteries, unable to pray, neither the prayer upon retiring
for the night nor the Eighteen Benedictions. All his
thoughts were about the match.

Sometimes he tried for months or even years, but
Tzalka never despaired. Now and then he was fortunate,
as when he arranged a match for the daughter of a certain
rich man. This man was a snob and rebuffed a townsman
who sat among the lowly in the synagogue. But then the
rich man became destitute, while the poor man grew
rich. It was easy then for Tzalka to implement the match,
and he saw this as God's handiwork.

Many Hasidim, too, conjectured that Tzalka was
blessed with special powers; that in issues in which he
had a voice, Providence favored him.

Tzalka was not averse to savoring strong spirits, but he
was never intoxicated. The community never reproached
him for his habit, they were aware that directly after a
round of drinks he became voluble about Holy Writ. He
then opened a Talmudic tract, and his melodious sing-
song echoed through the House of Study.

But there was one matter in which Tzalka was helpless
and inept: that was the handling of money. He did not
know how to open the purse of an uncouth and niggardly
rich man, because he maintained that hankering after
money was in general Satan's snare. And he did not yield
to Satan. And sometimes he said that if he were to
concentrate all his efforts and prayers to arrange a match
primarily for the sake of money, then he was likely to
come to grief.

When his efforts for implementing a match reached an
impasse, Tzalka resorted to a novel expedient: he started

reciting Psalms. And he did so silently, surreptitiously, for he knew that if people found out they would laugh at him. For Psalms are recited only when a person is at death's door, and not for the sake of potential new-lyweds.

It cannot be said that all the matches brought about by Tzalka bore a charmed life, but by and large they were fortunate. The affluent sons-in-law, those for whom Tzalka had provided beautiful brides and who had thus become partners of wealthy men, never forgot him. They presented him with something or other for the Sabbath and other holidays, and so did their brides.

He was perturbed by only one thing: there was a lack of bridegrooms who were Talmudic scholars. They were in great demand, and he looked high and low for more. True, Tzalka still had a reserve of fine young men, good providers who were skillful artisans and craftsmen, but he went about his task half-heartedly, when the candidate was not learned in Holy Writ. The quintessence of a match for Tzalka was a scholarly bridegroom who devoted himself to the study of the Torah and its related commentaries.

Tzalka was not the type of matchmaker who was through with his efforts when they led to a betrothal. Not at all. On learning that the lack of a promised dowry proved to be a stumbling block in consummating the marriage, he picked up his umbrella and visited the moneylenders to confer about a loan for the dowry. And when Tzalka "vouched" for someone, credit was extended immediately, and the wedding followed.

The community often wondered about Tzalka's success in arranging a match. But few knew that Tzalka's supplemental service in obtaining a loan for the dowry—and occasionally for the wedding expenses, too—was an important factor.

Even after the marriage of a couple, he didn't consider his mission accomplished. He kept in touch with them, from time to time, until the first child was born. And when he was invited for the circumcision rite, and especially when he was honored by being invited to be the godfather, he was overjoyed. Then, having downed a few extra drinks, he repaired to the House of Study, to pore over a tract of the Talmud. Only then did he consider his mission as a matchmaker accomplished.

The most arduous chore for Tzalka was to venture out of town. From time to time he had to travel to neighboring cities, for the town was too small for him to earn a livelihood. For him preparing for a journey to another city was like preparing to go to America. He took along his prayer shawl and two pairs of phylacteries,* as well as—to make a distinction between the sacred and the profane—overshoes and underwear for the winter season. Out of his notebook he copied pertinent information concerning the potential bride. For Tzalka, a bride was never ugly.

During his visit to a neighboring city that could boast of more erudite scholars and wealthier merchants, he tended to disparage them, maintaining that the best of them could not be compared to the lowliest of his town. So, his offer of a potential bride from Wyszkowo had to be considered as an extraordinary bargain that anyone should jump at blindfolded.

And if one of the natives ventured to ask if the potential bride was one of those liberal-minded damsels who, God forbid, frequent a library, and so on, Tzalka flared up. "Sir, do you know with whom you are dealing? If not, I beg your pardon. Find out who Tzalka the matchmaker is

---

*Orthodox Jews alternately don two pairs of phylacteries—one according to Rashi, and the other according to Rabbenu Tam.

and what kind of matches he makes, then you won't have to ask such absurd questions."

There was only one thing that could soothe Tzalka's anger: booze. One sip from the goblet and he became loquacious, and praised a scrawny lass as if she were a noblewoman and a princess the likes of whom could not be found in Poland, inferior only to Queen Esther and Rachel the Matriarch, to whose beauty the Torah and the *megillah* testify. No other girl could measure up to the "bride from Wyszkowo."

Silver-tongued Tzalka spoke in glowing terms about the affluence of his townsmen for whose daughters he was trying to find bridegrooms, and it was difficult to resist his arguments and recommendations even though they did not conform to reality. He had been an active matchmaker for many years, and no one had complained about having been cheated all the years he was an active matchmaker.

Tzalka hardly ever bore a grudge against anyone, particularly not against a poor man. Even when someone defaulted in paying his matchmaker's fee, he did not bring a lawsuit before a rabbinical court. It was a different matter when some haughty parvenu dared to offend him. He did not square accounts with the man right away. He was angry and bided his time, hoping to retaliate in the future.

Time passed. The offender all but forgot about the incident. At an opportune moment Tzalka—all excited—dropped in on the parvenu and shouted, "Reb Mekhel, I've got a young man, a veritable treasure. The moment she sees him, she'll be swept off her feet."

"Who is this young man?"

"Reb Mekhel, how can I tell you when my throat is dry?"

The host served drinks and a snack, then asked, "Well, Reb Tzalka, let's hear about the young man."

Meanwhile, Tzalka sampled the various brands of liquor, thinking how good it was to give the nabob his comeuppance.

The host was champing at the bit. Tzalka then asked, "Reb Mekhel, perhaps you have a pinch of snuff."

Handing him the snuff, the host said, "Well, let's hear about the young man."

"He is from out of town."

"What's his name?"

"Eliezer."

"His father's name?"

"Reb Itcha."

"What does the young man do?"

"A shoemaker."

"Get out!" the host screamed.

Reb Tzalka was already outside, relishing the thought of his retaliation for the past indignity.

Tzalka provided little for his own household. But he made due provisions for his offspring. His three adult children would not have to pay a matchmaker's fee. But they urged him to give up his calling and become a businessman. Tzalka turned thumbs down on that, arguing:

"One doesn't change horses in midstream, nor does one discard an established trade. What am I to do in my old age? Become an elementary school teacher? Do I have the patience to deal with teenagers? Am I to become a grain merchant—as if there weren't enough already in our town? As to earning a livelihood—well, God is bound to help!"

THE BOY

He was named Yekhazkel, after his grandfather on his mother's side. When he was a child he was called by the diminutive name Khatzkala. But during his adolescence he was nicknamed "the boy." Perhaps it was because of his size, or because he was quiet and pensive. In any case, hardly anybody paid attention to him. Whatever he said was brushed aside, like the uttering of some stupid youth. Things had come to such a pass that everything he did was disparaged. "Just look at the 'gentleman,'" people teased him; "What girl would ever marry such a boy?"

All this teasing engendered an inferiority complex in Khatzkala. He was sullen and disheartened.

Nevertheless, at the age of eighteen, Khatzkala became engaged to a girl from a reputable family. The bride was the opposite of the bridegroom. She was stately, athletic, full-breasted, and had dark glowing eyes. The event was considered a miracle.

When he first caught sight of her, Khatzkala was astounded. He couldn't believe that such a stunning woman was to become his wife. He thought that the merit of his grandfather's patrician lineage, which reached him like a golden chain from rabbis and sages, had stood him in good stead.

Sarah Gittel, the bride, on the other hand, when she laid eyes on the "man" to whom she had been betrothed, felt that her hopes were dashed. Holding back her tears, she brooded, "I am doomed to a life of misery."

Her maiden dreams about being loved by a stalwart groom now vanished as she had to embrace her childlike husband. More than once, she wished that her husband would curse and swear at her—even torture her—rather than yield and defer to her so readily.

Indeed her marriage to Khatzkala proved a great disappointment. Her desires were unsatisfied, they dissipated like a fog at the crack of dawn, but she was deterred from demanding more by her pride.

They had children despite the suppressed emotions. Sarah Gittel devoted all her love to the youngsters, caressing them and fondling them—and guarding them like the apple of her eye. Her devotion and affection were cherished not only by her children but also by the entire community.

According to the agreement Khatzkala's father was supposed to provide maintenance for the newlyweds for a good many years. But the wheel of fortune turned and Sarah Gittel's father-in-law became impoverished. She realized that he would no longer be able to maintain them. She knew that Khatzkala was unsuited for business. So, without wasting any time, she assumed the yoke of earning a living. In addition to being a wife and a mother, she became the breadwinner. She opened a shop selling kerosene, bran, flour, sugar and other such necessities.

In time, she gained recognition among the merchants and, particularly, among the poor. She made certain that no Jewish household should be without chicken, fish and *hallah* on the Sabbath.

Instead of being called "The boy's Sarah Gittel," she now became "Sarah Gittel the Righteous," or "Sarah the Wise." People beat a path to her door, not merely for assistance, but also for counsel. She came to be regarded as the mother of the town. Even Khatzkala gained esteem because of her. That was her reward for her suppressed emotions.

But she didn't remain for long at the top. She fell ill.

She succumbed while lighting the Sabbath candles. It looked as if an angel had kissed her and fetched her to Paradise. The townsmen claimed that she died a righteous woman.

Her six orphans were left at the mercy of the winds. Observing the Mosaic Law—according to which a Jew must not remain for long without a wife—Khatzkala married precisely on the first anniversary of his wife's death.

Khatzkala's second wife was entirely different from Sarah Gittel. She was short, broad-cheeked, and with sunken breasts, and her tiny eyes were always jerky, restless, as though afraid of her shadow. She was always wrapped in thought. Though good-natured, she was at a loss as to how to care for six orphans. The household seemed to be without a rudder. But at this crucial point, Khatzkala suddenly went through a metamorphosis: he became father, mother—a tower of strength. First, he placed his oldest son, Yerachmiel, in the care of his father, who was certain to rear his ward an observant Jew. The boy grew up to be a great Talmudic scholar. The entire community was confident that Yerachmiel would turn out to be a genius and Talmudic savant. "He inherited his mother's brains," people would say about him in the prestigious Yeshivot. He astounded his teachers with his erudition. In the House of Study, where he studied with a group of older students, he exhibited such profound knowledge that they commented, "Yerachmiel will be either a Talmudic sage—or a great heretic. . ."

Once, when Yerachmiel sat poring over a Talmudic tract, Reb Tzalka, the matchmaker, came in and urged him to return home immediately, because he was about to be betrothed to the only daughter of the respected and wealthy Reb Shmerel Tuchman.

"How does the bride look?" Yerachmiel asked.

"How dare you ask how the bride looks!" Reb Tzalka remonstrated. "Talmudic scholar of the community, you have the audacity to ask about the bride's appearance? Can't you leave that to your grandfather?"

Yerachmiel shuddered. He was frightened out of his wits, sensing that his mother's fate was in store for him.

"Look how he trembles!" Reb Tzalka remarked. "You act like a child. After all, you are a lad of sixteen, and by the time you get married you'll be eighteen. Don't worry Yerachmiel: your grandfather chose a bride of an aristocratic family, of sages and rabbis, for you. So what suddenly got into you that you've got to know how the bride looks? Love comes after one is married. So what's the difference? Every man has to get married, that's written in the Torah. Your father didn't get to see your mother, either. So what, didn't they have six children? You just rely on your grandfather, and you will be blessed with a wife, a righteous woman as your mother, of blessed memory, was."

And that is how it happened. Yerachmiel was engaged that same evening. His father-in-law promised to provide perpetual maintenance for the newlyweds, so that his son-in-law could devote himself wholeheartedly to the study of Holy Writ.

The traditional betrothal ritual was performed, but Yerachmiel was apathetic, staring ahead, listlessly. Although he didn't get to see his bride, he had a premonition that she was not the kind he had envisioned. He wanted a fiancee as beautiful as a princess. Like the Patriarch Jacob, he was willing to serve seven years as long as his fiancee was to his liking. Even as a youngster, the relationship between his parents had made a strong impression on him. He had sensed that theirs was a wretched life—a life that he wanted to avoid at all costs.

A year after the betrothal Yerachmiel got married. He

trudged to the *huppah*, the bridal canopy, feeling as though he was being dragged against his will. A vision stood in his way. His mother, energing from her grave, admonished him:

"My son, don't let them mislead you! You must be in love. Don't be a victim the way I was!"

But Yerachmiel hardly regained his composure when the glass was placed on the floor in front of him. He lifted his foot mechanically and smashed it with his boot.* He was only conscious of the noise of the shattered glass. It didn't occur to anyone that this was an expression of anger and protest.

After the wedding ceremony in the courtyard, Shaina Rivka, his bride, took his arm tenderly. But just then Yerachmiel sensed his mother's tears choking him. The most anxious moments occurred in the newlywed's chamber. A barrier seemed to loom between them.

It was only in the morning that he realized that she was tall and scrawny, all skin and bones. She eyed him meekly, with due deference and sensed that he was not particularly enamored of her. And just like his mother, Shaina Rivka had to swallow her pride and demand her right. She was aware that unless they became husband and wife, she would incur disgrace and put her good name in jeopardy . . .

Yerachmiel felt sorry for her. He was at a loss to understand why he could not warm up to her. True, she was not as comely as he had hoped, but neither was she unsightly. She was gentle and tender and obsequious, and yet he sensed a dividing wall between them.

Two years passed, and there were no children. His in-laws realized that their daughter was distressed. They

---

*At Orthodox weddings the bridegrooms break a glass. This is a symbolic act to moderate the merriment of the event, by reminding the assembled guests of the destruction of the Temples in Jerusalem.

watched her wasting away. But she would not, God
forbid, think of slighting her husband in the least. She
endured her agony silently, without uttering a word to
anyone.

However, her father's heart sensed her anxiety, and he
decided to confer with the rabbi about getting a divorce
for his daughter.

The rabbi scrutinized the situation. After lengthy
discussions with Yerachmiel, he concluded that something hidden seemed to disrupt their cohabitation. He
counselled Yerachmiel to leave his wife for at least a
year, to travel far and wide, and get to know other people.
By then, he, Yerachmiel, was bound to realize that what
he was yearning for was to be found in his own house.

Yerachmiel accepted the rabbi's counsel, and wandered through towns and villages. He earned his livelihood as an elementary teacher. And the more people he
met, the more he realized that he had no clear idea of
what he wanted.

Once, when he arrived in a small town, he found that a
cousin of his, who had been condemned by the family
because he had disgraced his parents, was residing there.
He had abandoned his Talmudic studies and become a
blacksmith. Yerachmiel recalled that the name of that
cousin was always whispered so that the children, God
forbid, should not hear it.

Yerachmiel was amazed to find that his cousin the
blacksmith was also a Talmudic scholar. He was astounded by the artistic and ingenious products that he
fashioned out of iron. He found loving-kindness in his
cousin's family. The atmosphere was serene, ideal; a
blend of Torah and manual labor. Yerachmiel unbur-
dened himself to his cousin.

"As long as you continue to eat bread you haven't
earned, you will be miserable," his cousin said.

Yerachmiel was ashamed. His cousin was right. "I

make all sorts of demands of others, while I contribute nothing. I don't even provide for my wife," he said. He recalled King Solomon's aphorism, "Wasn't the prophet Amos a shepherd?" And the *tanna*, Reb Johannan—a shoemaker? He examined his cousin's work. He could never attain to such craftsmanship. His hands were too frail for the blacksmith's task. But he had an idea that was bound to change his life.

He was a changed man when he returned. He could not look his wife straight in the eye. He kept to himself and hardly uttered a word.

Shaina Rivka was baffled by her husband's peculiar behavior. Who knows to what extent he was corrupted, she reflected. As he continued to be uncommunicative on the second day, she burst into tears.

Unable to endure his wife's anguish any longer, he approached her and said quietly, "Shaina Rivka—why do you cry?"

Whereupon his wife cried even more.

"Shaina Rivka, stop crying and I will tell you something new. Shaina Rivka, I want you to become my wife."

"Am I not your wife?" she asked, looking at him in disbelief.

"You are indeed. But according to the Mosaic Law, I am supposed to provide for you out of my own labor," he went on fitfully. "I want to go away, away from your father's house. Far away—past borders and oceans."

"With me?"

"Of course, with you. Not to be a recluse."

They embraced and both broke down and cried. Tears that had been pent up for a long time now ran copiously. Their anxieties were alleviated. That same evening they entered her father's room.

"Father, we wish to leave your house," Shaina Rivka let fall timorously.

"Whereto?"

"To Eretz Israel."

"What?" the old man screamed and broke into a hacking cough. "What are you up to now, Yerachmiel? Before, you were angry at your wife, then you went into exile for a year. What will you think of next? After all, as my son-in-law, I promised to support you for the rest of your life. Do you doubt whether I will be able to maintain you and my daughter? Don't you find my house prosperous? Are you lacking for anything here? And now you are asking me to take leave of my daughter, so that she may go so far away with you?"

After a pause the old man resumed. "True, that will be ours, with the advent of the Messiah. But my son-in-law should become a peasant? A tiller of the soil?"

However, Shaina Rivka sided with her husband and was willing to accompany him to the remotest corner of the world.

After considerable discussion the old man realized that he was up against a stone wall. He rationalized: who knows, maybe the plan is not so far-fetched after all? And he yielded.

Yerachmiel now became more loving with his wife. She was prettier, and her voice was more mellow. He envisaged a new, delightful life ahead of them.

With much hope, they left for Eretz Israel.

THE IRON BENCH

The foliage on the crests of the apple trees had begun to unfold. The sprawling meadows and fields burgeoned with flowers of every color. The rays of a warm spring sun sparkled on the Bug River, which rippled and washed the shore.

On the other side of the river, close to the forest, between two big pine trees, there was an old iron bench. No one could figure out whose idea it had been to set up an iron bench in the woodland. The peasants of the neighboring village referred to it as "Lawa Poniatowskego," as though it were an antique from the Poniatowski era. No one dared to move the bench from its moorings, and hardly anyone sat on it. Peasants, weary from a lot of walking or from hauling heavy wood, avoided sitting on it. The villagers were wont to relate different legends and myths about the iron bench, about how it wept at sunrise, how drops of blood trickled from it.

But once while strolling through that area I caught sight of an old man seated on that bench, his head resting on his hand. He sat listlessly, oblivious of the surroundings. He was unshaved and unkempt, and his garments were crumpled. I was debating with myself whether I should ask the old man what hurt him. But as I drew closer, he looked up at me startled and asked, "For whom are you looking here?"

And before I had time to reply, he went on, "Do you have a letter or some news for me, by any chance?"

I was taken aback for a moment. What did the old man want from me? Was he in his right mind?

I was sorry for not having avoided him. But I summoned courage to ask, "What news or letter do you expect and from whom?"

"From whom?" he repeated. "There's only one person from whom I can expect anything. I have no other friends in this world. Tell me—did she give you a message for me?"

"But about whom are you talking?" I asked.

The old man told me to sit down. I didn't want to do so, but his eyes begged me and I sat down at the edge of the bench, so that he could not reach me with his hand.

He gradually regained his composure. He was no longer consumed by curiosity. And my suspicion that he was mentally unbalanced also diminished. At the same time his voice changed, it was tender and sentimental like a young lad's.

"You are young and so beautiful," he began. "Your eyes are full of kindness. You stirred up memories of my youth. I, too, was young once upon a time. I was in love and dreamed of a happy life. I could have had daughters of your age today. But I remained an old bachelor, who lost happiness right here on this bench."

I shuddered at his words. My heart beat faster. What else was he going to tell me?

The old man then got a thick notebook out of his pocket and, moving a little closer, asked, "Can you read Yiddish?"

"Yes."

"Then read what it says here."

Finding beautiful calligraphy in the notebook, I asked, "Who wrote this?"

"Once I encountered a man with long hair and a faded cape on this bench. He looked like a musician, a poet, or a monk. He used to come here in the morning to listen to the chirping of the birds. He had Job's patience, and I told him everything. The last time I saw him, he gave me this notebook."

This is what was in the notebook:

"Once upon a time, Urka, the shoemaker's son, and the beautiful Sonitchka—Reb Hayyim Zaidler's daughter— sat on this bench and embraced.

"She was always here before him. Now and then, she waited near the iron pillar of the bridge, so that she could not be seen from a distance. And when he came, she flung herself into his arms. He was fond of the serene countryside, the river, the green meadows, the shore, the small thatched-roof shacks with their smoking chimneys, dotting the horizon. And when Sonitchka hugged him, he felt as though they were a part of the pine forest, and the banks of the river.

"Reb Hayyim Zaidler, Sonitchka's father, was a local financier and timber merchant. He transacted business with the gentry, and he adopted some of their patrician ways of life. He had maidservants and stewards, and he drove around in a magnificent carriage drawn by two thoroughbreds, and driven by a coachman. He had a well-groomed beard, and he was always greeted with an affable 'Good morning, Reb Hayyim!'

"At the other end of town, in a dilapidated shack, far from Reb Hayyim's grandiose house, at a workbench crammed with shoemaker's paraphernalia, a man and his son sat on three-legged long stools repairing shoes. The shoemaker's wife was busy in the kitchen, fussing around a steaming pot of mutton and potatoes.

"Ever since Urka had met Sonitchka, he was restless and high-strung. He had been working with his father for many years, and they just about made ends meet, and barely afforded finer garments to wear on the Sabbath.

In the last few years the father noticed that Urka was impatient on his stool, and he quit work long before sunset, and after washing up, he asked his father for pocket money.

"The father could not stand this. He was indulgent when he bought trousers or chamois high boots. A lad who frequents the library has to dress decently. However, to ask for pocket money on an ordinary Wednesday— that's a horse of a different color.

"Unlike his father, his mother was a saintly woman. She managed to save a few gulden from their meager earnings, and whenever her husband refused him, she gave her son a little money. She noticed a radical change in her son's mood. It was rumored—and Mindel, the fisherwoman had sworn to it—that Urka was courting Reb Hayyim Zaidler's only daughter.

"Spruced up in new high boots, starched white shirt and trousers with front pockets, like one of the gentry, Urka went out for a stroll on the Sabbath. When Sonitchka caught sight of him, the barrier between the patriarchal Reb Hayyim Zaidler and the lowly shoemaker vanished.

"The forest was serene and fresh. There were dewdrops on the berry sapplings. Birds twittered and darted about overhead. The trees seemed to breathe deeper through their thorn-lungs. The echo of a song was becoming more audible. It occurred to him that as long as he was with Sonitchka, the melody came from inside him. That is why he didn't say anything. He thought about the brochures that he had given her on their last rendezvous in the forest, pamphlets that one had read surreptitiously. He seemed anxious to find out whether she read them at all, and if she found them interesting. But that was merely a ruse. He wanted to talk about a gnawing pain that he had for the first time. But he didn't, because no sooner did Sonitchka enter the forest than she changed completely. She was no longer the Hasidic aristocratic young woman, who avoids looking at a stranger. She was exhilarated and she was singing a song. And he loved her singing so!

"He was astounded by the change in her, and he yearned to talk to her about it. But he didn't know how to put his thoughts into words.

"She wanted to play a practical joke. So she said, 'I'll bet that if your father does not consent to my becoming your bride, you'll forget me completely.'

"Urka was taken aback by her words. He stood up and, taking hold of her slender hand with his muscular ones, said in a quivering voice, 'I can swear to you that if I fail to marry you, I'll remain an old bachelor!'

" 'Is that so?' she giggled, reassured by his boundless love for her.

"A breeze from the river cooled her flushed face. As she crossed the bridge, the stream under her now was clear and rosy, it was as if a glowing sun's rays flushed her face. She paused for a moment to watch the waves. She was delighted, and it occurred to her that she could play with Urka indefinitely, if only she were not afraid of her father."

*　　*

"Sonitchka returned home a bit late, when the candles were already lit, and her father had performed the Havdalah ceremony.

"Reb Hayyim Zaidler sat down at the table, lit the extra bright lamp, and got out the huge account book, dotted with Rashi script (rabbinical characters). The ledger was his treasure. It recorded the number of logs that were hauled from the forest, the wages due the lumberjacks and the laborers in the sawmill, small sums advanced for liquor, and outstanding debts. When Rivka, his wife, came in, he mumbled under his breath without looking up, 'What about the thing that we were discussing?'

" 'I mentioned it to Sonitchka, but she made a wry face and was rather irritated.'

" 'I, too, am irritated. All I find is debts and more debts, and I still don't see a valid hundred-rouble note,' Reb Hayyim snapped.

"Rivka was accustomed to her husband's outbursts. She let him go on without responding.

" 'Rivka, are you ready to welcome our future in-laws?' Reb Hayyim demanded.

" 'Everything is ready. And if they were to stay for the Sabbath, there is a double portion of *tcholent*,' she said.

" 'Have you straightened out the matter with Sonitchka?' Reb Hayyim asked, removing his glasses.

" 'Why shouldn't she agree? For one thing, you've already talked to the young man and found him eligible. And there's not a shadow of a doubt about the lineage. So, as soon as our future in-laws arrive, Sonitchka will be congratulated with a *mazel tov*.'

" 'Meanwhile there are rumors that our daughter is involved with a fine bunch!' Reb Hayyim pursued.

" 'What?'

" 'It is said that Sonitchka associated with the "union villains" who aim to dethrone the Czar,' Reb Hayyim explained.

" 'Well, you're the father—you'll know how to handle the situation,' his wife heaved a sigh of relief. For a moment, she had imagined the worst.

" 'Call Sonitchka,' Reb Hayyim ordered.

"Confronting her father, Sonitchka sensed immediately that her parents must have learned of her love affair. Her father scrutinized her angrily for a moment, then shouted, 'I don't want you ever to meet that shoemaker's son again! Did you hear me?' "

While I was reading the notebook, he sat without saying a word. But the way he stared made me uncomfortable, and I had to stop.

"Do you show this notebook to everybody?" I asked.

"No."

"Then why did you let me read it?"

"Because—because when I saw you from a distance, I imagined Sonitchka was approaching."

"Pardon my asking, but what makes you come to this bench?"

After a moment's silence, he said, without looking at me, "I come here in the spring. My heart tells me that she will return. She can show up any minute! When I sit here undisturbed, Sonitchka appears. I caress her beautiful head that is covered with fresh dew. I adore her gorgeous eyes. And I seem to get more youthful and handsome. I am not what you see now."

I wanted to return the notebook to him, but he pleaded, "Hold on to it. It is the story of a human life."

He got up, gazed at me with a silent farewell, and trudged off into the forest.

I remained alone on the bench, clutching the notebook.

A SOVIET SOLDIER

On the day it was reported that the Red Army captured Odessa, the few guests who happened to visit with us were in a good mood. One of them, a slight woman with a snub nose and amiable smile, proposed to tell a story about a Red Army soldier. After the guests were seated around the table, she began.

"It happened in the First World War. It was a hot summer day. The sultry atmosphere was filled with fumes of chloroform, pitch, and blood. The sky was overcast, it thundered now and then, and it looked like a storm about to break.

"For the past two weeks the nights had been calm, though one could still hear the echo of occasional gunfire. Exhausted by the troublesome events, the inhabitants of the town that had been captured by the Bolsheviks, relaxed and believed that salvation was near. There were no longer pogroms. True, arrests were on the increase, people were taken into custody by the Bolsheviks for selling food products and on the dual suspicion of anti-Bolshevism, especially former proprietors, a term which was the equivalent of exploiter.

"The community was deluged with paper money. Gold, silver and copper coins were as rare as hen's teeth. The Red Army was shopping for all kinds of consumer goods, from fur coats and boots to women's underwear, combs with glittering stones, ribbons, and what not. And they didn't bargain. Jews began to deal in foreign currency. No wonder when one could get a basket of paper money for a small silver coin.

"My younger brother, who was twelve years old, had been twiddling his thumbs since the schools had been closed, envied the neighbors who were trading their commodities for loads of bank notes, and he decided to engage in business. So he got hold of a parcel of cigarettes and made his way to the marketplace.

"A sergeant caught sight of him trying to sell his product, took him into custody and escorted him home—that meant he was under mother's arrest. The little fellow, not realizing the danger, pointed to mother. The sergeant was about to take her to the commandant. Mother argued that she was innocent, hoping to be spared the arrest.

"I was seventeen then, and was working in the City Hall. During the war I had attended Polish as well as German schools, and being bilingual, and having had some experience under the Polish authorities, I was called upon to render services to the Bolsheviks.

"As the sergeant was about to arrest my mother, the order came that the Bolsheviks were to retreat. The command was so unexpected that even the confidential records and documents had to be left behind.

"When I learned that the Poles were advancing, which meant new hostilities, I was frightened, and hurried home to be with the rest of the family.

"We lived in a small modest wooden house in the suburbs, in the vicinity of several Gentile families. Our alley was quiet. The acacias in our little garden filled the air with fragrance. The townspeople were already visibly worried. Women carrying infants and baskets of food were running for shelter. Old people and invalids struggled to get away.

"I arrived home full of fear, but my mother was overjoyed to see me and said to the sergeant, 'This is my daughter.' Though desperate at first, she had regained her composure and was saying that her daughter held an important post with the government, so that she could not be accused of treason.

"The sergeant turned to me and asked why I allowed my young brother to engage in trade. I explained that I could not be held responsible for the actions of a youngster and that I didn't even know what my brother was doing. When I told him that his own commandant had already fled, and that the Poles were advancing—he rushed out.

"Shortly after that, a hooligan came into my room, where I was all alone, and tried to rape me. I tried to ward off the malefactor, and finally he said that I should give in to him. He contended that he could rape, but preferred not to do so, although I was nothing but a damned Jew.

" 'Do it, or I'll shoot you like a dog!' he shouted.

"An explosion shattered the windowpanes, toppled the furniture. I fainted, and the hooligan ran.

"My mother and some of our Gentile neighbors came running, and she screamed, thinking that I'd been shot.

"When I regained consciousness, I saw that I was on the earthen floor, with my mother and younger brother beside me, crying. In the other corner the Gentile family was kneeling before a crucifix, over which a little red lamp burned.

"Outside there was a cloudburst. The sounds of thunder mixed with the bursts of the cannons. Roaring fires lit up the sky.

"The fighting continued for a few hours. Then someone knocked on the door and announced, 'The Bolsheviks are back!'

"People emerged from their hiding places, families were reunited, and volunteers attempted to extinguish the fires with buckets of water.

"As I was hauling a bucket of water with a neighbor's

son, I came upon two bodies, one was the hooligan who had tried to rape me, and he was dead; the other was the Red Army sergeant, still alive. He looked at me with glazed eyes and whispered, *Golubushka, Golubushka—ya umirayu* ('Little dove—I'm dying'). He told me that he saw the hooligan trying to rape me and he shot him. Then a bomb exploded near him. He begged me to put an end to his life with his revolver.

"I wept but could not tear myself away. I thanked him and wanted to kiss his hand. I did not know what to do.

"A few moments later the sergeant shuddered and breathed his last."

The slight woman was lost in thought.

THE FOREST TELLS A STORY

On one side of the little town there is the Bug River, which is a tributary of the Vistula. On the other side there is an ancient evergreen forest with sandy hills, a region noted for its healing effect on tubercular lungs. The primeval woodland rustles and tells stories. It recounts stories about revolts, insurrections, in the time of Chmielnicki;* and about bandits who used to lure their victims into the jungle; and about the meditations of Hasidic youth; as well as about broken hearts.

One thing the prehistoric timberland doesn't understand: why have nations fought since time immemorial? It passed from the Poles to the Russians, then to the Germans and back to the Russians, and finally to the Poles again.

But today the woodland roars in a special way: not only the trees, but our people, too, are at the mercy of the wind. Blood is spilled recklessly! The earth is saturated with it. Might supersedes right! Battles rage and the "chosen," the Jews, are the scapegoats.

The woods are noisy. And if you understand this language, you know that they say the following:

"When Kaiser Wilhelm's Germans occupied us along with the town, they didn't spare the Poles either. They shouted 'damned Jew!' as well as 'Polish swine!' And you, little Rachel, whom it knows as a sensitive soul because

*Bogdan Chmielnicki (1595-1657), Cossack chieftain, who led the revolt of Cossacks and Ukrainians against Polish landowners. In 1648, he launched terrible massacres annihilating hundreds of Jewish communities. That period is known as *gezerot tah ve-tat*. The Ukrainians regard him as a national hero.

of your frequent visits there, don't take the disparaging epithets of Kaiser Wilhelm's Germans to heart."

Little Rachel regained her self-esteem. It was not the Jews alone who were hated. Now she looked her young Polish classmate straight in the face. At one time he held her in high esteem; but when he thought the Jews had gained in status, or to put it another way, the Gentiles had been taken down a peg or two, he avoided her. He could not be reconciled to the thought that they shared in the punishment meted out by the Germans. He was chagrined at the fact that Rachel could communicate with the German conquerors in their language, while he was stymied.

Rachel worked as an interpreter for the new government, and rendered special favors to the community. She granted an exit permit, issued an extra bread-ration card, and so on. She remained as unpretentious as ever, but her classmate failed to recognize her kindness and modesty. He envied her since she, a Jewess, was promoted to such an important position even by the Germans.

The wheel of fortune turned. National flags changed hands and the young Pole got his commendation. Poland was liberated. There was boundless joy, people were embracing in the streets, church bells pealed, wine flowed like water and, along with the wine, Jewish blood. The battle cry "Beat the Jews!" merged with the Polish hymn.

Jewish hearts understood the Polish drumbeat. Ominous days set in, days of harassment, persecution, and dreadful pogroms. Rachel was disheartened. Her Polish classmate put on the eagle hat at a jaunty angle and enlisted in the army. He had forgotten about the high esteem in which he held her a while ago. At nightfall, when Jews go into hiding, he appeared and whispered to her that he would guard her house, and then he said something about lovemaking.

News of pogroms in the neighboring towns sent chills through the local community. And before long, the local Jews are pilfered, mugged, their beards are plucked and their shops broken into. And Poles threaten with even more dire deeds. The days and nights—especially the nights—are filled with anxiety. The scraping of a mouse or the shrill chirping of the cricket is enough to frighten a man out of his wits.

Those were grim, sleepless nights for Jews. The members of every household relinquished their beds and huddled in one corner, each trying to shield the other with his body.

From time to time, Rachel's Polish friend assured her of his vigilance and that in the event of an impending assault, he would paint a cross on the door. He believed that Polish blood flowed in their veins and that ultimately she would marry him and convert to Christianity.

One night the exhausted Rachel dozed off and in a nightmare she seemed to hear menacing steps, to see knives and spears and blood. She was awakened by a loud knock on the shutters. Certain that the dreaded curse was at hand, she grabbed a knife and decided to do away with herself rather than to submit to the blood-thirsty barbarians.

As the banging on the shutters became louder, her mother gathered her children and began to recite the *Shema*. Then Rachel heard a familiar voice, "Get up! Why are you still sleeping? It's *me*, Jan!" After some hesitation, Rachel plucked up courage to open the door. Whereupon her friend announced haughtily, "You over-slept. The entire community has been murdered including your old grandfather. But I saved your life, the way I promised you. You will be mine. Now you can see that I was serious."

Rachel fainted. All she remembered was that when she regained consciousness, she saw a doctor at her bedside, and her grandfather held her hand and her mother was weeping. Then she heard her Polish friend chuckling, "Ha-ha-ha, you silly goose! You allow a few words to upset you, and you pass out. My God, how frail you people are! Mere words can put an end to you!"

"You are right," Rachel responded. "And I am grateful for your efforts. But it is no use for you to risk your life for a Jewess. We are tired of a life for which we have to struggle eternally. Thank you for your chivalrous protection. But if the rest of us are doomed, I want to be among them. My life is no more valuable than the lives of my brothers and sisters and of all the other Jewish families. Now get out! I never want to see you again!"

Thereafter Jan kept away. That is the tale of the primeval forest.

A TOWN *(SHTETL)* ON THE BUG RIVER

The shores of the Bug River are dotted with small Jewish towns. The ancient forest, flanking the town, is at times verdant like the fresh grass of the meadows; at other times, it presents a somber, dark rampart. As one views it from the valley, it looks as though an old nobleman had stretched out in a lounge chair and leaned back.

The local children started out life, picking black and red berries in the forest, bringing home baskets filled to the brim. As the youngsters grew up, they set out for the forest at the crack of dawn, when the dew was still fresh, to pick hampers full of mushrooms. But it was when they became adolescents and were animated by youthful zeal that the forest found a new role.

The forest attracted the young because no one interfered with their privacy. Scores of couples felt free to embrace, without any interference.

Political dissidents met there secretly to devise strategies for an uprising. It was safer there than at home. Yeshivah students walked to the forest and took secular literature out of their long kaftans, which they read without the Orthodox headmaster's interference. The more frequent their visits to the forest, the shorter their kaftans became, and the curly sidelocks that were tucked behind their ears were soon combed straight.

The forest could also terrorize. It was a hideaway for bandits who swept down on Jewish merchants returning from a fair.

In the autumn, the forest served the town. It provided dry boughs, branches and logs for the winter. Men and women hauled the bounty home. The generous woodland never forgot the impoverished, and when the first gusts struck it, shook off the dry twigs that had accumulated under the evergreens.

The woodland also restored ailing lungs to health. The aroma of evergreens rejuvenated them. In the summertime people from all over the land flocked to inhale the healing fragrance of the tall pines, which were so broad and thick that a man could not reach around their trunks. They seemed to care for their wards like dedicated nurses.

On the south side the forest extended to the very banks of the Bug River, but the latter was never at peace with the forest. In the summertime its sands were heated by the sun, and they burned any sprout that fell there. But on the other side, the river lost its natural appearance. A part of the shore was paved with stone, and after the river overflowed, green moss grew between the stones.

In the wintertime the river was transformed into a long bridge. Frozen solid and covered with snow, it served as a thoroughfare for sleighs and wagons, and people took short-cuts across the ice.

But in the spring the river woke up with a roar. Its frozen center cracked and shattered, and then its water crested until it inundated fields and villages, dragging along stables and barns with the livestock, ricks of straw and hay, and stacks of wooden logs from around the village houses.

The water of the Bug River was potable. Water carriers used to deliver it to many households. In the summertime women used to wash laundry on its banks. Bathing in the river was a tradition which the children were the first to take advantage of. There was hardly a youngster who could not swim. Now and then, the river turned ferocious and claimed a victim. During the *Sefirat ha-Omer*,* Orthodox Jews refrained from bathing in it. Only after the river had already exacted its toll did they bathe.

On Rosh Hashanah, for the Tashlikh ceremony, the entire community smoked the pipe of peace with the river, exonerating it of its past misdeeds. After all, it had its many advantages. Observant Jews emptied their pockets of whatever trash was in them. The river good-naturedly accepted the ejected transgressions and carried them ever so far from the town.

Two bridges, one wooden, the other metal, spanned the river. The one made of wooden planks linked the town with the pine woodland on the other side. It was always bustling with pedestrians, going to or from town. Occasionally, a few Hasidic young men appeared on the bridge, ostensibly to bathe, but they were drawn to the forest that they knew was full of lovers, where they thought they might encounter a beautiful girl, for whom they would be prepared for any sacrifice, as Jacob was for Rachel. They would even remove the long kaftan, the way Jacob removed the heavy stone boulder from the well.

Several trains crossed the iron bridge during the day. Here footsteps did not echo as on the wooden bridge. And it was not dangerous to cross it on foot, because the train signalled its approach. From time to time, young couples slipped by here at twilight, to avoid detection.

The railroad station added to the hustle and bustle. It crossed a large orchard. On both sides, there were green benches for the weary traveler. The big platform ex-

---

Sefirat ha-Omer, the precept to count 49 days from the day on which the Omer was first offered in the Temple until Shevuot. The Bible states, "You shall count off seven weeks. They must be complete."

tended up to the tracks on which trains rushed in huffing and puffing. Between trains, silence reigned there. Then, with the arrival of a train, the station woke out of its deep sleep. Its walls with the dusty windows trembled, and fidgety passengers began shoving and pushing toward the exit.

The station was more appealing at night. The blazing headlights of the locomotives illuminated it in the nocturnal gloom.

Passengers with their suitcases and bundles sat on the rickety wooden benches. Along one of the walls there was a buffet with a big simmering samovar. Gentry, officers, and other officials pontificated in the exclusive room, which smelled of hard liquor and spiced sausage.

From the station to the town there was a short distance that people generally covered on foot. Nonetheless, there were coachmen with coaches and droshkys, earning their livelihood by transporting passengers to and from the station. Occasionally, the coachmen feuded and even came to blows over who had rights to a fare.

In the winter the station was snowbound, with only a narrow path open to it. The interior was cold and damp from the snow on the passengers' boots. Sleighs, filled with hay and blankets, arrived with their bells ringing. The nags halted in their tracks, their hides shuddered, their nostrils covered with hoar-frost, their ears pricked up. Having discharged his cargo the coachman clucked, and the nags turned around and headed for home.

Zalman Mekler, a young man who had relinquished his father-in-law's assistance and struck out on his own, kept close to the station. This was his sole source of income. He catered to visiting merchants who in the winter were in search of rabbit and skunk skins, and in the summer he carted visitors afflicted with respiratory ailments. His pockets always bulged with such objects as packs of matches or the "Rabbi's Lottery," etc., the things passengers asked for.

On the Sabbath the area around the station was deserted. The horses in the stables rested from the week's toil. The station looked weary and languid. No coachman set foot in this region. The cashier peeped out of the grated porthole and yawned loudly. And if someone did approach to buy a ticket, the cashier eyed him angrily as though the latter intended to disrupt his rest. The railroad cars passed through half-empty, and the passengers en route were too listless to raise their heads to look at the deserted station.

Nearby, on the highway there was a big glass-works which radiated a great deal of heat. Orthodox Jews asked for forgiveness as they passed it and observed, "If such heat comes from a structure fashioned by human hands, how much more terrible the heat must be in Gehenna!"

The highway became more deserted as it left town. The shacks along the way were hidden by a sea of grass.

Two streets ran parallel to the Pultusk highway: one, the "Oplatkes," was unpaved and dotted with peasant houses and barns. In the summertime, this area smelled of fresh milk. Workingmen and maidservants strolled along it and whispered sweet nothings to each other. The other, the Synagogue Street, led to the big Retkess orchard where fierce watchdogs pounced on any intruder. Poor Jewish families, handicraftsmen, artisans and vendors, making the rounds of the villages resided in small wooden houses outside the town. The street ended at the courtyard of the House of Study, the Ger *shtibbel*, and the ritual baths. The bathhouse attendant, the sexton, and the gravedigger, in a separate shack, also lived there. One could see the black hearse. There was also a small handcart which was used to haul and to sell yellow sand for sprinkling the earthen floors of the dilapidated Jewish houses, and thus relieve their gloom.

The last street led to the Warsaw Road, which ran up to the iron bridge with the railroad tracks—and that in turn linked the villagers to the rest of the world.

At some distance from the iron bridge there was the Soloway Palace, the relic of an old Russian official. The palace was surrounded by a big orchard, which was the favorite promenade of the young intelligentsia. The pharmacist and the physician and a few wealthy Jews lived nearby. There was also a sawmill. From there byways and detours led to the small villages and the estates of the gentry.

The Warsaw Road ran into town near the butcher shops. The butchers and their apprentices squatted on discarded butcher blocks. On the opposite side there were a few scattered shops on the edge of the marketplace.

The marketplace was the center of life. Fair days were held there every Tuesday and Friday. The inhabitants regarded the location as the salient place in the community. It was nicknamed "Street."

"Are you headed for the Street? Are you coming from the Street? Do you reside on the Street—or on the highway?" That's how they talked about the marketplace.

The marketplace was surrounded by one- and two-story houses, most of which had cellars and were thus known as cellar-houses. These were inhabited by bakers and their families. The upper floors were occupied by traders who had their shops in the marketplace, and by craftsmen, particularly tailors and dealers in old clothes, who on fair days displayed their goods on makeshift stands.

The shopkeepers in the marketplace, with few exceptions, were Jewish. They dealt in all sorts of commodities, catering to the townsmen and villagers. House utensils, metal products, toys, scythes, hand tools, dry goods, provisions, and so on. Artisans and women vendors who had no stores used to display their wares on makeshift stands and stalls in two rows, facing the marketplace. Sometimes vendors quarrelled over a potential customer.

Wintertime the town was tied hand and foot. The shopkeepers and vendors were attired in their winter *matuvkas*, or padded Mackinaw coats, and used fire pots to keep warm. Now and then, a padded garment, generally a petticoat, caught fire. People came running and wrenched the burning skirt off the woman.

The marketplace bordered on the street known in Polish as Przedmieście, one section of which was inhabited by impoverished Jews and the other by impoverished Gentiles. At the end of this street were the imposing buildings of the Post Office, the Courthouse, and the City Hall. Beyond them, and surrounding the town, was a magnificent landscape and forest.

On the other side of the marketplace several small streets led in different directions. Among them, Fish Alley was the most interesting. With its dilapidated small houses, it appeared to be asleep. But on Friday, or on the eve of a holiday, Fish Alley came to life. There were washtubs filled with live fish. The fishmongers and their wives, the women shoppers looking over one washtub after another—gave the place a unique atmosphere.

Life in the community proceeded calmly and even monotonously. For days and weeks on end it seemed as though the merchants stood in front of their shops, eager for a customer; and women hawkers gathered to gossip, as though in a trance, hesitating to wake up the community. Even the apprentices in the workshops hardly hummed, and when they did so, you could not hear it outside. Even the teen-agers, who were everywhere on fair days—on other days plodded soberly to the *heder,* where they studied listlessly.

Things were at a standstill in the community until fair days. Then, at the crack of dawn, peasant carts hauling farm products streamed to the marketplace. Tradesmen from the neighboring towns arrived with wares which they displayed on stands. Other visitors strolled through the marketplace looking for merchandise. The entire community, young and old, teen-agers and apprentices, seemed to participate in the activities on a fair day. The worshippers rushed through their morning prayers, gulped down their food, and headed for the marketplace. The community was excited. It made its living on those fair days.

When the fair day was over, life once again became calm and monotonous. But on that day the townsmen had their hands full, without a moment to spare. The housewives set to work cooking, cleaning and preparing for the holy Sabbath. But the marketplace was the center of activity from sunrise to sunset.

"Fetch this for mother in the marketplace."

"Go to the marketplace and tell father to come home and eat."

"Deliver this parcel to the marketplace."

The business dealings and huckstering would have dragged on until nightfall, as was the case on other fair days, if it weren't for the sexton, who suddenly appeared in the marketplace and in a mellifluous voice shouted:

"To the synagogue! To the synagogue!"

And the marketplace vanished as if by magic. The stands and stalls were cleared and everything was hauled into the shops and nearby houses. The shops were closed without further delay. And even the peasants stopped drinking, hurried to their carts, and headed for the villages.

The sun set and the town became peaceful. Even the

scramble to and from the ritual baths seemed to echo, "Just be patient and you'll see how peacefully we live. Our hurry now is in honor of the holy Sabbath."

And before long Jews, in their festive attire, were streaming to the synagogues and the Houses of Study to welcome the holy Sabbath. Candles could be seen through the partially-curtained windows. Everything was ready.

On the Sabbath afternoon, following the repast, Hasidic young women sneaked out to saunter off with young men to the forest.

"Where is Bluma?" a mother would ask.

"Most likely in the forest," someone replied.

On that afternoon, Yeshivah students took examinations in Orthodox homes. The Aramaic of the Gemara was interspersed with Yiddish and articulated in melodious sing-song. Girls eavesdropped outside and sometimes peeped in. Catching sight of an examiner pinching the cheek of a student, they went away giggling, implying fondness for the lad.

Life, not just of the Jews, but of the non-Jews as well, even in the adjacent villages, was tranquil, unruffled. It may have been the placid river and the forest that shielded the town from an evil eye.

On Sunday, Church Street was teeming with Gentiles on their way to church for prayer. Near the church, young men were looking at the innocent, God-fearing girls, clutching their prayerbooks. Church bells were pealing. The street became deserted. The singing of the choir and the priest's sermon reverberate outside.

In the morning, Church Street was calm and sleepy again.

Jews led a peaceful and more or less happy life until the intrusion of new events.

It began with the occupation of the German

Wehrmacht during World War I, bringing a little renais-
sance, with the starvation. A library was set up in town
for the first time. Various political parties were formed.
There were social gatherings, and a struggle between the
old and new generations. The local rabbi, along with the
Orthodox group, became a political power, and tried to
stop the cultural events. The rabbi excommunicated the
parents who allowed their adult children to go strolling
in the forest. On the Sabbath the rabbi stationed a guard
near the bridge to prevent the desecration of the Sabbath
by walking beyond the *Techum Shabbat.** However, the
young generation forged ahead toward enlightenment
and culture, undismayed.

But before long, they ran into a new stumbling block.
The Poles now wielded authority. Though both Poles
and Jews had lived in the region for generations, the
moment they had power, the Poles persecuted their
neighbors, the Jews, beating, robbing, plucking their
beards, and finally killing them.

The Jewish youth left. And as soon as they set foot in
another country, they made plans to bring over their
relatives.

But the town still teemed with Jews, who observed
the Sabbath and other festive occasions. The primeval
forest continued as the sentinel of the community. It was
taken for granted that black clouds came up from behind
the forest and that the loyal guardian of the town, the
forest, roared to warn of an impending storm.

But once this loyal guardian failed in its mission. No
one had anticipated that misfortune would swoop down
so unexpectedly and spare neither the elderly nor the
infant in the cradle.

Techum Shabbat ("Sabbath limit"), an ancient law restricting observant
Jews to walking no more than 2000 ells beyond the confines of the community.

It happened in September, when golden rays cavorted on the Bug River. The fields had just bestowed their bounty on the community, filling the granaries, and the fruit trees were laden with apples and pears. The sky was serene. The forest was quiescent, and did not portend any trouble. Suddenly steel birds swooped down out of nowhere, bombing the defenseless towns, wreaking great havoc. Shortly after, ferocious swastika-bearing barbarians invaded the town, slaughtering Jews, razing Jewish homes, as they sang the Horst Wessel song.* Jewish blood colored the Bug River.

The primeval forest shuddered. One evergreen roused another, and lashed out with its needles. It seemed as if the forest wanted to run to the town, to rescue the little Moishas, and Shloimas and Hannahs and Rochels, whom it knew so well, and to shield them, as it shielded hunted animals.

But beside the primeval forest, no one cared.

---

*Horst Wessel song, the official song of the German National Socialist (Nazi) Party.

ON NEW SOIL

BEFORE THE HOLY ARK

Rabbi Adler had been in a state of excitement ever since the new synagogue was built. Designed by noted architects, both inside and outside this splendid house of worship was lavishly decorated.

The synagogue was in a suburb that was becoming a center of Jewish life. Two decades before no one would have imagined Jews becoming established in an area of meadows and marshland that appeared more suitable for a golf course then for a housing tract.

The Jews had settled here to escape certain ethnic groups who were crowding them out. They came from the heart of an industrial metropolis where they had maintained houses, shops and businesses for generations. Here and there a synagogue had been abandoned and converted into a church. The Jewish mansions on Chicago Boulevard gradually passed into other hands, as their former proprietors joined the exodus to the suburbs. A newly built highway contributed to the rapid expansion of a new settlement.

The town that came to be known as Southfield looked much like any other well-to-do residential section in America. The houses in Southfield were especially attractive with their sloping roofs, their spacious drawing rooms, the plate glass windows looking out on newly planted saplings and shrubbery. A small stream flowed behind the rows of houses, which were set among small gardens and flower beds. There were spacious garages with electrically operated doors. Yiddish was not to be heard in the quiet streets. But on entering a house, an

Alef-Bays diagram, a pair of silver Sabbath candlesticks and a Chanukah *menorah* on a sideboard would be visible. In some houses, the children knew a few words of Hebrew.

With the influx of more Jewish residents, new houses went up and the price of the once relatively inexpensive plots of ground began to go up.

The synagogue that towered in the neighborhood was huge. One wing included classrooms that could accommodate more than a thousand children; the other contained the rabbi's study and his large library of books in English, Hebrew and Yiddish, the three languages in which he was proficient.

A visitor could not but be impressed by the furnishings of the study, the heavy mahogany desk and the crowded bookshelves. But still more imposing was the rabbi himself—the tall, slender figure, the bony face with the trimmed beard which suggested that of a patriarch. Even while he was still a student he had been known as a philosopher.

The day was bright and sunny. Daylight poured through the big windows of his study, cloaking the spiritual leader with silent radiance. He had come in early with the expectation of a visit from two clergymen of another faith with whom he was on friendly terms.

Before long his secretary announced: "Bishop Marius and Pastor Gala are here."

He rose to welcome them and soon, as was the custom, the three were engaged in a discussion. Though they represented different faiths, on one point they were in accord: that God is the Father of all creation.

Bishop Marius, a Roman Catholic and a native-born American, did his best to reconcile the authority of the Church with the personal liberty in his homeland, which he had come almost to deify.

As the three men gathered around the rabbi's desk, their discussion reflected the tensions of a city torn by racial disorders, and made uneasy by layoffs in the automobile industry.

The Christian clergymen paid close attention to Rabbi Adler's learned observations, interposing brief comments of their own from time to time. They had come, in fact, not to carry on a discussion with the Jewish philosopher, but rather to listen to his commentaries.

"We American Jews are duty bound to help American society understand the basis of our common search for peace, freedom, and independence," Rabbi Adler was saying.

"But we must find a common cause that will unite us and allow us to join forces," Bishop Marius observed.

"I think it is the desire of man not to be alone in the world; there is yearning in him for a supreme authority, a universal spirit, that unifies mankind," said Pastor Gala.

The two clergymen paused, waiting for the rabbi to answer.

"There is something more mighty and universal. If there is one experience that is shared by mankind, it is the experience of suffering." The rabbi paused for a moment, then went on: "There is an old story about this. A patient in Naples once complained to his doctor about being subject to despair: he could not get rid of a lingering melancholy. The physician said, 'I suggest that you go to the theater. Carlini is giving a wonderful performance in a comedy; he makes the audience roar with laughter. Go and see Carlini. His performance and his jokes will help you shake off your melancholy.' The patient then burst into tears: 'But *I am* Carlini!' "

The story struck a sympathetic chord in his guests. Whenever they met Rabbi Adler, they profited from his erudition and his commentary on abstruse theological problems. On this occasion, once again, they came away rewarded.

The rabbi escorted them out and waved good-bye as they drove away.

On their way home, as the two men shared their impressions of the meeting, Pastor Gala recited a few lines from a poem by the rabbi:

When mercy is removed from me,
Shall I cry out where is my God?
Lying in a bed of pain, shall
I forget His past blessing of health,
Or that even now he grants me life?
In sorrows shall I forget
The joy, the laughter, the delight
That have been my lot in life?
Or when days are dark
Shall I forget the light
Of former days?
Oh God! Give me the power
To rejoice in gifts
Of former times.
Though now gone from me,
Let them live again in my memory.

Bishop Marius was silent. It was only when they reached their destination that he said, "It would appear that you are under the rabbi's influence."

"I even quoted him once from the pulpit. But you, Father, have said nothing about the poem," Pastor Gala observed.

"I was deeply impressed by it," the bishop replied.

"What impressed you especially?"

"Simply the idea that we ought to thank God for everything. That is the keystone of faith. That is a splendid insight," the bishop declared.

Rabbi Adler had likewise been pleased with the meeting. For him, neither solitary thought nor written discourse equalled the spoken word. The living exchange between one person and another, the living thought that was expressed—the "oral Torah"—were for him the pillars of human spiritual attainment. Even though words faded into the void without an echo, nevertheless the spiritual essence, the reverberation of the hidden thought so that the ears could discern it, became a manifestation of spiritual radiance.

Tired being alone in his study, he went to look in on the classes at the synagogue day school. He had great hopes for the children. He felt a special kinship with their generation because of its leaning toward religion and because their mother tongue was English, his own native language, in which he was more at home than in either Yiddish or Hebrew.

He took in the joyful faces at a glance, with special attention to one boy whose name was Richard. Since early childhood, the rabbi recalled, this youngster had shown special inquisitiveness concerning things that were beyond his years. The rabbi was accustomed to Richard's strange questions. Today the boy asked, "Rabbi, I want to know whether you can share God with anybody."

Behind the childish naivete of the question, the rabbi discerned an urgent motive. After some questioning, he learned what Richard's purpose was: He wanted to pray for a Christian friend who was ill, and who according to reports of other children, had gotten no better despite special prayers by the priest. But he was afraid of calling down the anger of the Hebrew God by imploring help for an uncircumcised one.

"Dear child you must know that all people are God's creatures," the rabbi told him. There is the sublime exhortation in Leviticus (19:18): 'You shall love your neighbor

as much as yourself.' God did not say, 'You shall love a
Jew as much as yourself.' It doesn't matter whether your
friend is a Jew or a non-Jew so long as he is a decent
human being."

Richard left in an exuberant state. The rabbi, suppos-
ing that the youngster had simply wanted to talk with
him, would have dismissed the incident from his mind
had it not been for what followed.

Before leaving the synagogue Rabbi Adler happened to
pass by the Holy Ark and was puzzled to see that its
curtain was moving. Coming closer, he found young
Richard murmuring a prayer for the recovery of his
friend, unaware of the rabbi's presence. That discovery
left an indelible impression on the rabbi.

Years passed, and Richard became a student at the
university, where he demonstrated great intellectual
ability. His professors were occasionally astonished by
his comprehension of complex social and psychological
problems, and by insights that were those of a genius.
They could not fail to notice that his thinking was
influenced by the Torah. Despite the liberal atmosphere
of the university he remained dedicated to the teachings
of his rabbi. The principles of the Holy Torah continued
to guide his life.

The transition from the parochial school to the university had not changed his outlook. He remained the same
zealot of traditional Judaism. He compared modern
social science with the tenets of the Torah, and saw the
latter as the more just and humanitarian. The Torah
called for the release of a Hebrew slave after limited
servitude; it set aside harvest gleanings for the destitute,
as well as tithes; it prohibited loans with interest, and
ordered the pawnbroker to return a pillow at sundown.

Several hundred Israelis were students at universities
in Detroit, and some of these were Richard's classmates.

He became a particular friend of one named Abraham Blau.

An assiduous student, Abraham Blau was a Sabra, a native Israeli. In their conversations he talked at length about his homeland and his homesickness for it. Like the rest of the Israeli students, he kept largely to himself and did not visit local Jewish families. When he was invited to some special occasion, he would find an excuse not to go. The local Jews were bitterly disappointed when this happened. They could not reach those students. An impossible barrier seemed to separate them. The young Israelis disapproved of the young American Jews because they "lived in luxury." For the Israelis, life had been hard; they did not drive expensive cars; their parents did not have enough money to subsidize their careers. But they were in much closer rapport with their own community; integrated with their home environment they shared in its joys and sorrows, its security and dangers, and were happier as a consequence. Richard was angry when Abraham told him that because of this he could not feel at ease in America. Richard tried to reassure him, telling him of his rabbi, whose fervent sermons in support of Israel were integral to his own faith. But Abraham raised objections to all of this.

Abraham came from a Hasidic family, and although he had moved with the times, he kept to the traditional practices. His mother had been born in Meah Shearim, the ultra-Orthodox bastion in Israel. His father came from Galicia.

As their discussions became more vehement, Abraham declared: "God, the Holy One, is in the Land of Israel. He doesn't feel comfortable in any other land."

"The springs of the Mosaic faith run clear in this country, too," Richard answered.

"The source of Judaism is in the Land of Israel. You must visit Jerusalem," Abraham persisted.

Abraham was a fierce opponent of the Reform Synagogue for slipping to Christian practices. For example, he regarded traveling on the Sabbath to worship as vulgar and profane.

"If we were to maintain that kind of discipline," Richard insisted, "we would lose the worshipper in the synagogue."

"We will discuss all this when you come back from Israel," Abraham said.

Shortly before his vacation Richard told his parents that he wished to spend the summer in Israel. Though they raised no objections, they were concerned about where he would live. Richard then explained that Abraham had recommended him to a youth group in Meah Shearim.

On his return from Jerusalem, Richard became critical of the fine synagogue building. Whereas once he had admired the sculpture of the "Burning Bush" in front of the Ark, he now looked askance at it. He was amazed to find that there were no Hebrew letters on the Ark. The traditional gold embroidery of rampant lions was missing from the curtain, and so were the Ten Commandments. How unlike what he had seen in Jerusalem! He was outspoken in his distress.

Nor was it the actual building that disturbed him most. It seemed to Richard that holiness was completely misrepresented here. There was something erratic about him. He was in a state of turmoil. One moment he spoke about religion, the next about the assassination of President Kennedy. He talked of prayer, and then of revenge. Revenge against whom? He could not have said. He declared that revenge itself is sacred—and revenge even, occasionally, is *Kiddush ha-Shem*, to sanctify the

Divine Name. He went into seclusion, avoiding contact with others, for days on end.

Aware of, and troubled by, their son's strange behavior, his parents consulted a psychiatrist. He did not rule out a pathological disturbance, but was at a loss to pin down the cause. He was inclined to attribute Richard's behavior to his extreme brilliance. "The young man is a genius—and genius sometimes borders on madness." Since he did nothing really bizarre, did not get drunk or act irrationally—and, above all, since no special therapy was recommended—his parents and friends were lulled into accepting the view that Richard was a prodigy.

When he learned that Richard had been to a psychiatrist, Rabbi Adler became especially concerned. During their frequent meetings, the rabbi had observed the confusion in the young man's state of mind. The rabbi then talked to some of Richard's teachers. His history professor said, "He is an intellectual with an original and speculative mind." Another professor said, "He yearns for philosophical absolutes, above all in the laws of nature. Yet as a genius he is aware that many philosophical issues have not been resolved." His professor of political science declared, "I have never had a more dedicated student. He is endowed with the highest academic ability."

Rabbi Adler was pleased to hear this praise. Nevertheless, he was worried. As he puzzled over Richard's case, he sensed that something was being concealed, that there were ominous tendencies which defied treatment, and that to restore him to lucid thinking would not be easy.

RICHARD'S REACTION TO THE KENNEDY ASSASSINATION

The assassination of President Kennedy affected Richard more than any other young man in the city. Avidly he read everything dealing with that tragedy. He stared at the photos and illustrations in the newspapers. At night especially, the event hovered before his eyes as though he had been a witness. At times he pictured himself standing near the killer as he aimed his rifle at the President's head; at others, he would see himself riding in the open car next to the beautiful Jacqueline. Now and then he reproached himself for failing to topple the murderer from his perch on the fourth floor, and thus rescue the President, whom he adored. Richard cherished Kennedy's youthful spirit, his gallantry, his courage during the war, and his diplomatic skill, and was grateful for the establishment of the Peace Corps and when the President disbanded it, he deplored the act, and was anxious to have it restored. In his imagination Richard addressed many letters to the President, trying to convince him of the necessity of the Corps.

After the President's life had been extinguished, Richard would sit listless for hours at a time. It was only when his reveries took him to Dallas, and he found himself in the company of Kennedy's assassin, that he became alert again.

Richard felt most at home when he was lost in dreams. In the mornings he went to his classes at the university, but his afternoons were nerve-racking. The situation eased by nightfall, when he once more argued with the murderer.

As the days passed, Richard had undergone a radical transformation. At first he had felt disgust for the assassin, both for his atheism and because he had killed a great leader. But as a typical American, in his imagination, he allowed the killer to plead his own cause. The more he listened, the more Richard found himself trying to penetrate the inner recesses of the killer's soul. Whatever flashed through Richard's mind did not dissipate, but settled into his subconscious and finally permeated his entire being. While he pursued his studies, he was obsessed by the one concern: the assassin.

After many exchanges, Richard concluded that the killer had himself been a victim who could have been saved, but to whose plight a self-seeking society had remained oblivious. The assassin told him that he was a fond admirer of the President, that he had been like a lover so enamored of his sweetheart that, suspecting her as she smiled or casually thought of someone else, he ends by shooting her.

Richard could no longer shake off the Man from Dallas, who had gradually won his sympathy. He had come to believe that he alone could be trusted with the assassin's secret.

"I am condemned by everyone," he complained. "Before I could say a word, a hoodlum from the underworld stepped in and pumped those bullets into me. That hoodlum never tried to understand me! Would he, would the world, have believed that I admired the President? How would you say it, Richard, in your academic vocabulary, that faith is absurd? That's it. Believe me, Richard, I didn't know what I was about to do? I was driven by obsession, by an overpowering force, to buy that rifle with the telescopic sights. I tried out the gun several times, and it seemed to me that the bullets went through my own heart. I felt that I was shooting my sweetheart."

Richard felt mesmerized by the situation, unable either to extricate himself from it or to understand it.

Once he walked past the synagogue and bumped into Rabbi Adler. "Richard! How are you getting along?" exclaimed the rabbi. "How are things at the university?"

"Thank you, rabbi, I am at home with my thoughts," Richard replied.

As the rabbi moved on, Richard stared after him for a moment. Then he was seized by a sudden insane idea: "He is the one!"

A cancerous thing now grew like an embryo in his mind. He was helpless before the madness that had taken possession of him. His grievances against the rabbi's liberal Judaism intensified. One night he sprang to his feet and exclaimed aloud, "This is my Kennedy! He is the one!"

Sometimes he fought off the terrible nightmare, but as the days passed, and he continued to be haunted by it, he was no longer in control of himself.

On the eve of the Sabbath he was exhilarated by the thought of what he was about to do. His unhinged psyche swung like a pendulum. Out of control, he was no longer a rational judge of his own actions, and had lost the ability to steer clear of danger. He slipped a revolver into his pocket and hastened to the synagogue, where he was to make common cause with his rabbi, his Kennedy. Together they would leave the synagogue and the community, and make their escape.

THE LION IN HIS LAIR

Expounding a sermon from the pulpit was Rabbi Adler's greatest pleasure. As a matter of fact, the congregation was far more interested in the spiritual leader's discourses than in the Sabbath prayers. His approach had always been philosophical, and his interpretations of the Torah were in keeping with the times. He never imposed duties or restrictions. In his sermons, he not only quoted from the Torah but also mentioned political and historical events.

On this particular Sabbath, Rabbi Adler had omitted the weekly Torah portion and devoted himself instead to the birthday of Abraham Lincoln. Concentrating on the historical events of the period, he held the congregation's attention. He was emphasizing that Lincoln was not murdered by a political enemy, but that he "fell as the victim of a maniac." At that moment a young man with dark blond hair leaped onto the pulpit. His eyes flashing with hatred, he screamed, "This synagogue is a den of hypocrisy and the rabbi is a desecrator of the Hebrew faith!"

The young man spoke in English, with a scholar's careful inflection. And he approached the rabbi without the customary gesture of deference.

The rabbi was stunned. The situation was frightening. Still, he did not lose his head. His first thought was that Richard merely intended to take issue with him in a public demonstration. But to do so in the middle of a

141

sermon! Such a thing had not happened in all his career. But now he saw that Richard held a revolver. His first thought was for the safety of the Bar Mitzvah boy who stood near by. Placing a hand on the boy's head, shielding him with his own body, he whispered, "Frank, get down from the pulpit."

Gesturing to the gabbai to leave the rostrum, he became calmer.

"Your interpretations of God and Godliness are deceitful and fraudulent!" Richard was shouting, "Your servility toward the Christians makes you an apostate, a traitor to the Torah and to the God of the Jews."

Rabbi Adler now ceased paying attention to the diatribe. He knew that Richard had gone mad. In the rabbi's contorted face there was compassion for the unfortunate youth. Stepping up to him, he looked into the muzzle of the revolver. Flashing through his mind was the terrible thought, "Is this the end?"

In the congregation, the ominous silence continued. The rabbi wondered briefly why no one intervened, why no one cried out. But then he realized that no one but he, as rabbi and mentor, could hope to reach the demented and threatening young man. While he tried to wrest away the revolver, Richard waved it threateningly and went on with the diatribe:

"You brought me to such a state of mind that I am ashamed to say that I am a Jew. There are men, women and children here who are self-seeking egotists, interested only in their careers.

"Your sermons about Judaism are nothing but heresy and iniquity! You are introducing false doctrine into Judaism. There can be no parceling out of holiness, no compromise in upholding the law of Moses. The Star of David and the Cross cannot be combined in the mutual service of God. Whatever you preach from the pulpit is deceit and fraud!"

The rabbi did not speak. Perhaps he feared that to do so would only provoke the young man. He drew himself up, hoping to stop the lunatic from going through with his drastic intention by gently wresting the gun from him.

Then something flashed before the rabbi's eyes. A shot echoed through the synagogue. The rabbi felt a sting in his arm, saw blood on his prayer shawl. He was still conscious. It was only after the killer had stepped closer and fired again, that the rabbi slumped to his knees.

The sound of that shot brought Richard out of his deluded state.

Taking in the scene at a glance, he was bewildered by what was taking place. Who had dared to make his rabbi kneel before him? But now, he saw the weapon, still smoking, in his hand, with the rabbi dying at his feet. Something tugged at his heart, and he felt an impulse to help the victim. He hesitated, aware now that the rabbi was dying. For a moment his sanity returned; he aimed the revolver at his right temple and pressed the trigger.

And so the rabbi and the student lay side by side while their blood trickled toward the Holy Ark.

A REFUGEE FROM PARIS

I used to meet her now and then, in the public square near my home, always at the same time. She was small, scrawny, dressed in black, with a black veil over her face. She reminded me of a mother mourning her son who was killed in the war. She sat quietly on a bench, playing with a string of black cord wound around her wizened neck and hanging down on her sunken chest. She sat all alone, staring listlessly ahead.

It was rumored that the old woman was Gentile and a refugee from Paris. She had relatives in the city. She had managed to come to America. I was anxious to get to know her, but I hesitated, fearing that she was mentally unbalanced. But once I caught sight of her face under the veil, and my suspicions were allayed. It was a grief-stricken face with sad eyes that had shed many tears. Yet I still lacked the courage to engage her in conversation.

Then an opportunity presented itself. A girl was pushing a carriage with an infant in it. A wheel slipped off and was rolling in the direction of the old lady. When it reached her feet, she was startled, got up and made an effort to put the little wheel back. She fumbled with her pale, bony hands and long fingers, but to no avail. The girl was busy calming the crying baby. I walked over and offered my help. Whereupon the elderly woman smiled and remarked in ungrammatical English:

"God sent you here." After a momentary pause, she added, "Who else can help us? God had deserted us, because we did not obey his commandments. We sinned a great deal. The men have been killed."

While watching me put back the wheel, she continued barely audibly:

"Don't you think that God is taking revenge? No, my child, we didn't sin that much. They will pay for everything—those accursed Germans: for the innocent blood that they shed, for the blood of our sons and daughters, and for the blood of the small children and old women, and for the blood of the Jews they slaughtered like sheep."

She fell silent, but did not leave. I looked at her and thought that she was demented by the trials and tribulations that she must have experienced. However, I decided to get to know her, and I asked her to wait until I was done with my task. The girl thanked me and was on her way. And the elderly woman and I sat down.

It turned out that she was not mentally deranged, but careworn and depressed by the ravages of the war. I was spellbound by her story, because she referred to the Jews with special affection, as though she herself were Jewish.

I was eager to hear more details about her life in Paris during the Nazi occupation. But she kept on recounting her gloomy reminiscences, ignoring my specific questions and comments.

She had witnessed cruel murders by the Nazis. But to watch the living was even more harrowing. She thanked God, who had granted her son courage to avenge the murders and to die like a proud Frenchman. He was captured, but he put a bullet through his head. His last words were: "The French will be a glorious nation again; love, freedom, fraternity and joy will return."

Tears trickled down her hollow cheeks when she mentioned Jean. Her proud son could not endure the subjugation of Paris. His frail father was dragged by the Nazis to a concentration camp, where he died of torture. She was grateful to the Lord for having found his body in order to bury it alongside Jean's grave. Father and son now lie in the same grave. And what will become of her? Will she some day be buried alongside her dear ones?

Following Jean's death, the Nazis confiscated her magnificent estate, confining her to a small room. Unable to find peace of mind there, she roamed the streets during the day, returning home only for a night's respite.

"Would you please tell me something about life in Paris at that time?" I pleaded.

But she went on talking about the untimely death of her son. She told me that he was religious and was fond of reading the Bible. He admired and revered the Jewish people, and he suffered when he saw how so many innocent Jews were massacred. Occasionally, he wore the yellow star,* and he always walked arm in arm with a Jewish friend. He joined the underground, taking revenge on the enemy—and he perished in the attempt.

"Yes, I am already familiar with all that," I let fall.

"Do you have many Jewish friends here?" the old lady suddenly asked.

"Of course, I am Jewish," I answered.

"You do, indeed, look like a saint," she whispered, leaning toward me. "You are pale and your dark and beautiful eyes are aglow, with Jewish kindness and sadness. And your lustrous black hair, and your intelligence and bearing! Oh, how my Jean would have rejoiced at meeting such a woman!"

"I'm sure, there have been—and still are—many beautiful and intelligent young Jewish women in Paris," I commented.

"That is true," she nodded.

She was lost in thought for a while. It was a sunny day.

---

*Under the Nazis the Jews were compelled to wear the yellow "Shield of David" badge with the letter J, or the word Jude inside it.

The square was bustling with children playing and amorous couples.

"The woman must be mentally ill from her gruesome experiences," I thought and was about to leave.

"Please stay a while longer," she said, taking my hand. Then she added, "Let us go and pray for my son's soul. Take me to a synagogue. I want to pray to the Jewish God. How Jean loved the Bible!"

"Very well," I said. "Let's rest a while longer, and then we'll go. There is a synagogue not far from here."

Suddenly the old lady fell on her knees before me, weeping and imploring me to forgive her, because she along with all the other Christians was guilty of the crimes against the Jews. She went on to say that all Christians are to blame for the atrocities that the Nazis had perpetrated against the Jews. She said something in French that I didn't understand.

"Madam, please get up!" I pleaded.

Curious spectators gathered around.

"What's going on? Did anything happen to the old woman? Why is she crying? Is she a relative of yours?"

Within a few moments she was on her feet. She sat down and said to the onlookers, "It's nothing at all. Please leave us alone."

The curious crowd departed, one by one. The old lady lowered her head and fell silent. I got up unobtrusively and left the public square.

I wondered about the fate of that old lady for some time, spoke to friends about her, and hoped to see her again, and take her to a synagogue, where she could pray to the Jewish God. But I never saw her again.

THE MOTHER

At the end of summer I vacationed at the home of a Jewish farmer.

The early mornings were pleasantly cool. The dew on the grass glittered in fantastic colors at sunrise. Later, the autumn sun showered its golden rays on the fields, the tree crests and the rooftops. It was like that throughout the day. It was as if the sun wanted to say goodbye to Mother Nature for a long time, for the winter. The nights were quiet and starry. Nearby the murmur of a stream echoed like the whispers of a lover. On such nights one sleeps well, not as in the city.

A roadway passed near the farm, leading to the railroad station. The golden fields were already stripped bare, the grain had been harvested, and sheaves covered the fields. Now and then, a shepherd led a flock of black and gray sheep to pasture. Cattle in the barn chewed their cuds, longing for the meadow. Farmers carried full cans of milk, and their air was redolent of a myriad of aromas.

Here and there the multicolored kerchief of a woman flashed. Sunburned, carefree children played. The fragrance of freshly harvested hay hovered in the air. Bumper crop and serenity held sway.

But the atmosphere in the home of the farmer was grim. The household was cheerless. The reason was that their only son, a young soldier who had come home on a furlough, was about to rejoin his unit. His father accompanied him to the railroad station and, as they took leave of each other, the father urged him to give a good account of himself in the struggle against the Nazis.

His mother and I escorted him to the railroad station,

which swarmed with men in uniform and a few people in civilian dress. There was a great commotion. The atmosphere was charged with suspense. Everywhere eyes reflected nostalgia, longing and hope.

When the special railroad car opened its doors to the enlisted men, the mother of this soldier pleaded with the conductor to let her into the car, so that she might spend a few minutes with her only son. She stressed the fact that after all he would be fighting for all of us—and who knew if she would ever see him again.

The conductor, a tall, corpulent phlegmatic man with a walrus moustache, was adamant.

At first, she exhorted him with dignity because she was not used to begging, but thwarted, she changed her approach, remarking, "Aren't you aware of what's going on in Europe? Don't you know? . . ."

The conductor scrutinized her for a moment, then he yielded.

The grateful mother scanned the crowd and when she caught sight of her son, rushed over to him, and embraced him. And as he was about to leave, she said:

"My son, be brave and give a good account of yourself in the war against the Nazis, who have murdered millions of our innocent men, women, and children. My son, my son . . ."

And as the train pulled out, the mother stared ahead with glazed eyes. Her face with the pug nose was grief-stricken and her thick lips were quivering. I thought she would collapse at any moment and be trampled by the shoving throng.

I took hold of her hand, trying to console her. She was startled, then apologized, a bit embarrassed.

"It is difficult to be brave at such a time. After all, he is my only son and he is such a noble soul, and a dear friend."

"He'll come back," I consoled her.

But she was oblivious to my words. Lost in thought, she went on as if to no one in particular:

"He was planning to marry a girl with whom he was in love, and now—. He left a diary, in which he recorded all their meetings. He used to read excerpts to me; he confided some of a young man's secrets to me. But what am I jabbering—what's become of me? Well, it cannot be any other way! Who else is to go out to fight the Nazis? Oh, God, who?"

I feared that the situation was affecting her mind, and I escorted her down from the platform. I felt a special kinship to her, because one common fate was now uniting all mothers, sisters, and brides. We walked around, and she kept talking about her son, until it was time to return to the farm.

She led me into her son's room and pointed out the playthings and other knickknacks of his life. Then she showed me an album of photographs of him and his friends and his fiancee. She stroked each object with tenderness. She opened a closet, observing that all his clothes would remain undisturbed, for objects also have souls and nostalgia. His bed with the red woolen blanket, like everything else would wait for him. She had given birth to him, heard his first outcry, and later on heard him utter his first word. His cradle stood in the corner. She recalled that he had been critically ill more than once, and that she had always saved him from death with her boundless love. God, who would watch over him now?

"God will watch over our sons now. We will be victorious," I said.

"Of course, of course," the mother chimed in, gazing at me with her sad eyes.

She was reluctant to leave the room. When it got dark, she turned on the light, got out his diary, and read me about some of the young man's joys and sorrows, and about her, his mother, whom he loved very much, and about his classmates and all the sensations and adventures of a precocious youngster living on a farm. Then she turned to the pages dealing with his love affair, holding back her tears.

"I think you're right to be proud of such a son," I interposed, trying to calm her.

Her husband knocked on the door, exclaiming, "That's enough! Let our guest eat her dinner!"

But after the repast we returned to her son's room, where she resumed talking about her brave son on his way to avenge the Nazi slaughter of his people.

At night, I could not sleep. I saw the farewell of the mother and her son headed for the firing line, and I heard her message to him. What a remarkable woman! What a wonderful Jewish mother!